THE WRONG TIME TO TALK ABOUT LOVE

New York was a small town for Jerry and Jenny. Everywhere they went they ran into each other. In no time at all, they had fallen in love. The only decent thing to do was to tell Jenny's husband. But what can you say to a man with a knife in his back?

MELVIN SIMON PRESENTS
A MARTIN POLL PRODUCTION

FARRAH   **JEFF**
FAWCETT-MAJORS   **BRIDGES**

SOMEBODY KILLED HER HUSBAND

Co-starring
JOHN WOOD   TAMMY GRIMES   JOHN GLOVER

Music Composed and Adapted by ALEX NORTH

Written by
REGINALD ROSE

Produced by
MARTIN POLL

Directed by
LAMONT JOHNSON

A COLUMBIA PICTURES RELEASE

Somebody Killed Her Husband

A NOVEL BY CLYDE PHILLIPS
FROM A SCREENPLAY BY REGINALD ROSE

A JOVE/HBJ BOOK

Printed in Canada

Library of Congress Catalog Card Number: 78-68175

First Jove/HBJ edition published August 1978

I

The Village was just waking up.

Bleary eyed men pulled their robes tightly about them as they braved the chill November morning long enough to find the *New York Times* on the front stoop, and their wives reluctantly pulled open the drapes to welcome yet another drab day into their living rooms. Entire families waged daily wars over bathroom supremacy, and only those residents who lived alone enjoyed an extra five minutes of peace before venturing onto the cold tile and praying for enough hot water for a decent shower. High rents and hot water have little in common.

The supers dragged overflowing trash cans between the buildings, making more than enough noise to awaken the late-sleepers. The cans scraped broad white lines in the cement before clanging together in a heap by the curb. The earlier carpool riders waited by their front doors, constantly peeking through the thick glass to look outside as another car double parked and honked twice in the universal signal that vaguely resembled some sort of urban mating call.

Schoolkids tumbled out of their brownstones, the youngest with their faces obscured by woolen mufflers and heavy hats pulled over every exposed inch of skin by doting mothers who years ago had sworn they would never treat their children this way. Many were dressed in the raggedy-chic styles of their liberal parents. Overalls and tennis shoes, sweatshirts and corduroys were the uniforms of the day, of the generation. They headed south for their three blocks' journey just past the fire station to the elementary school. A confusion of school bells and fire alarms had long since become a way of life to the youngsters of Greenwich Village. The older kids, the boys with their jackets defiantly open and the girls chattering in gossipy huddles, moved west to the high school and junior high that faced each other across the small park that consisted of little more than a few benches, a fountain that only had water when it rained and a lawn-bowling green where the ninth-graders hung out at night to practice spitting for distance.

It was a fact of life in this neighborhood: They did their time at the junior high, paid their dues. And three years later, they inherited the privilege of crossing the park every morning and passing time in the bigger building for another three years before assuming the place reserved for them in front of the pharmacy on the corner. Then followed a summer of blissful hanging out until N.Y.U. or Dad's business, or another, more lucrative enterprise beckoned. Anything, as long as there was something constructive to do come September.

A few doors from the pharmacy stood one of the few buildings in the area that had not yet been refurbished. Slouching like a poor relative between two newly painted and shingled duplexes was Mrs. Calamesa's house. She'd owned the place for thirty years. Her kids were born there and her husband had died there. She had similar plans for herself and wasn't about to pour any more money into the dump than was deemed necessary by the city's Health and Safety Department. She had also managed to master the questionable feat of living with four cats and one huge German shepherd under the same roof. Collectively, they clung to their meager existence of disrepair and noise with a useless arrogance.

The neighbors could do little more than bitch and openly pray for the day that Mrs. Calamesa would join her husband and lower the property values in the here-after.

Years ago, the third-floor attic of the building had been fashioned into a small, one bedroom apartment for her oldest son. But he had complained too much about the lack of heat, and windows that never quite closed all the way, so she'd had him evicted.

The place remained vacant for many months until a quiet young man noticed the three-by-five card on the bulletin board at Kaplan's Grocery and, against the advice of everyone in the store and complete strangers on the street, he decided to check it out.

Mrs. Calamesa adored him at first sight. His bright and honest thirty-year-old face, his full, dusty blond hair, quiet blue eyes and modest, unassuming manner simply knocked her out as soon as she opened the door to his timid tapping. He was so unlike her own son that she was thrilled to have him move in right away.

So, Jerry Green had come to Greenwich Village.

His apartment was a carefully ordered disarray of used furniture and ancient appliances. An old door balanced across two sawhorses dominated the front room and served as a dining room table, an ironing board, and most importantly to him, a desk. A lumpy green couch that swallowed those foolhardy enough to actually sit on it occupied the back wall beneath two chrome-framed prints. One print was a signed and numbered lithograph of that season's American Ballet Theatre poster and the other was a starkly impressionistic rendering from the 1972 Munich Olympiad. Broad, freshly stained overhead beams concealed a well-positioned track light system, and the ceiling sloped gently toward a deep bay window that overlooked the street.

Except for the table and the couch, the rest of the room was tastefully, if inexpensively, decorated with a few mismatched chairs, some valiantly struggling plants, and several more neatly framed prints.

A series of richly painted, but precariously suspended bookshelves lined the entire wall to the left of the front door. Stereo components and a reasonable selection of classical recordings and middle-of-the-road rock and roll albums were symmetrically arranged in the center. From there, a collection of a couple of hundred paperback books, interspersed with an occasional hardcover, spread their way to the ceiling and outward to the edges of the shelves. No spectacular titles here; just the usual array of academically and socially required reading of a child of the Sixties. Hemingway to Sartre to Koestler to Vonnegut and back again to Fitzgerald.

One section of the shelves was a bit incongruous. The entire bottom right quadrant, some five levels in all, was packed full of manuscripts. Some were reams of pages in brightly colored boxes, others were stacks of sheets in manila folders secured with rubber bands and a few more were bound in looseleaf folders. Titles for each were carefully written with a black felt-tipped pen and if one were to look closely, it became evident that the manuscripts were perfectly arranged in alphabetical order. Jerry's very private treasure.

Next to the telephone on the worktable, a black goose-necked drafting lamp was vise-gripped to the corner and another partially completed manuscript sat beside an old Underwood typewriter. A sheet of white paper curled around the roller as if awaiting instructions, and two bottles of crusty correcting fluid rested in a cigar box full of paper clips and postage stamps.

A steam iron rested, unplugged, on its heel on the collar of a soft blue workshirt. Next to it, a compact cassette tape recorder whirred softly as its microphone was activated in the other room. The extra-long mike wire ran from the machine down to the floor, past the couch, along the short hallway and over a pile of dirty clothes into the bathroom. The sound of running water and Jerry's animated voice travelled back along the wire and mingled in an obscure muddle on the tape.

Jerry stood on a towel in front of the bathroom sink and splashed hot water onto his face. "Dig a lot deeper into Charlton's motivations," he said into the microphone that hung loosely around his neck on a slender black cord. "Why would he rather be an inchworm? Um . . . inchworm . . ." He paused to consider this as he spread a glob of shaving cream over his face and neck. "Make a note, check the children's book department at the store to see if inchworms turn into anything more stately in later life . . . I never heard of it." He rinsed his hands and turned off the water, having long ago learned to preserve that precious commodity.

"Nah . . . Cut the whole inchworm thing altogether." As he shaved for a few moments in silence, it occurred to him that he wasn't crazy about the name he was using for the main character of his latest book. "Charlton. That sounds too faggy." Stopping for a second to hitch up his boxer shorts and catch a rivulet of shaving cream that was meandering toward the mike, he worked the name over in his mind. "Charlie, Charles . . . nope. Uh, Chadwick. Chilton?" Putting the razor down on the edge of the sink, he removed the mike from his neck and looped it over the toothbrush holder to the right of the mirror. Then he proceeded to shave under his chin. Slowly. This was traditionally his most tender spot and he scraped away at the light stubble gingerly.

Temporary inspiration struck home and he stopped. "Chester! Chester the caterpillar!" Jerry smiled and winked at his brilliant self in the mirror. But, upon reflection, the smile faded and he mused, "No, wait. Chester's the goddam cricket who kept singing the sextet from Lucia in the subway station."

Leaning toward the mike he said with final determination, "Okay, the hell with it. It's Charlton!" Just as

11

he went to finish off the last tiny speck of shaving cream, Jerry nicked himself in the spot where he'd nicked himself once a week since puberty. The white shaving cream turned a pale pink and then a bright pastel red as his blood found its way to the surface.

"I'm bleeding. Charlton is out!" He reached up and switched off the microphone.

By the time Jerry finished dressing his wound with a patch of toilet paper, he was running behind schedule and had to hurry to make it to work on time. Pulling on a pair of tan slacks and brown loafers, he searched his closet for his favorite shirt. Then he remembered. Scurrying to the living room, he grabbed up the soft blue shirt from the desk, put it on and went to the hall closet. He pulled a dark blue tie from the inside doorknob, quickly fumbled it into a knot and threw on the coat to his tan suit. After making a silent promise to water his plants as soon as he got home, he slipped the tape recorder into his inside coat pocket, and fumbling with the mike cord, hurried from his apartment.

He took the steps two at a time, not caring about disturbing Mrs. Calamesa at this hour. At the bottom landing, Jerry stopped to pull himself together before opening the heavy front door and facing the day. From inside his landlady's flat came the sound of Bruno, her leviathan dog, scratching steadily at the door while several cats gave forth with a whining concert of morning contrariness. But Mrs. Calamesa ignored it all as she sat bug-eyed and happy in front of her television set, a tall glass of hot tea and milk on her lap. It was nine o'clock, time for her favorite show. She was in love with Stanley Siegel; Bruno would just have to wait.

Jerry pulled open the door and scooted down the stairs. When he reached the sidewalk, he turned to his right and strode briskly past the accumulated trash cans toward the corner, his hands plunged deep into his pants pockets. At the corner pharmacy, he turned right again and made his way past the Village night spots, jazz

12

clubs, and coffee houses closed up hard against the unfamiliar daylight.

The book shop at the next side street was just opening as Jerry walked by, lost in thought. Removing his hand and the microphone from his pocket, he switched on the recorder and spoke softly. "Carter Caterpillar . . . no . . . Cary." He paused for a moment, the mike at his lips. Then he shook his head in disgust. "What Cary! I hate that . . . sure, with a sister named Lisa and they see their father on alternate weekends."

The sun was just beginning to poke through the cloud cover and he decided to forgo his usual subway ride and catch the uptown bus on Sixth Avenue. A few more minutes wouldn't make that much of a difference. There was only one other person at the bus stop when he got there: a boy about ten years old dressed in a blue blazer with matching grey slacks and sweater. Everything about him said "private-school-for-rich-obnoxious-kids." Under one arm he carried a soft leather book bag and under the other was the *Wall Street Journal*.

Jerry nodded diffidently and seated himself at the other end of the bench. "Calvin," he said into the mike. "Calvin. That's not bad . . . but does it have religious significance? Gotta consider that." He clicked off the tape and looked to the sky. The sun slipped behind a cloud and the bench was suddenly shrouded in shadows. Perhaps it would be better to think of another name.

The crowded bus groaned to a stop and Jerry followed the impeccably dressed kid on board. After dropping his fare into the box and smiling at the frowning driver, he began to weave his way toward the rear. Timing his steps perfectly with the lurch and sway of the rapidly moving bus, Jerry finally burst through the clogged midsection and found himself looking at an empty space on the long rear seat. But the rich kid had seen it too and Jerry could tell that the brat was going to make a try for it. So he did what any mature, normal adult would do in that same situation. He ran for the seat, sat down, folded his hands in his lap.

Seated comfortably between a huge black woman with a shopping bag clasped protectively between her feet and a short Puerto Rican man. Jerry turned his attention to recording his notes.

"So this book deals with an ecology-conscious caterpillar," he whispered into his hand. "And this caterpillar refuses to eat leaves or any other living green thing . . . and he gets hooked on liverwurst."

The man on his right tugged at his mustache and tried to watch Jerry from the corner of his eye. The black lady, not too crazy about riding next to people who talked to themselves in public, tried to slide farther away and nearly crushed the sleeping young executive-type against the window.

"That's very human," Jerry continued. "Also, he knows he'll become a butterfly someday. He'll be sipping nectar someday and pollinating everything in sight." He smiled at the image. "Good!"

Leaning forward in tandem, the black lady and the Puerto Rican man looked at each other across Jerry's body. Each raised an eyebrow expectantly, hoping for an explanation from the other. When none was forthcoming, the Puerto Rican gentlemen zipped up his jacket, rose and moved into the crowd to stand near the exit. Who needs to sit next to a nut?

An elderly woman with a tattered pink shawl spotted the vacant seat and was just about to make her way toward it when the rich kid swooped in from his place in the aisle and plopped himself down next to Jerry

Oblivious to the reactions of the other passengers, Jerry went on with his story. "Maybe do a half page on withdrawl symptoms in the cocoon." He lowered his hand as he gathered his thoughts. Then he raised the mike once again. "Question: Where does he get the liverwurst?" he whispered. "Also, how does he know he'll become a butterfly?" A pause. "He read it in an ency-

14

clopedia? No, that's crazy. Instinct. Right, talk a bit about instinct. Also, is liverwurst funny, or just quaint?"

The kid in the blazer turned to Jerry and, tucking his leg up on the seat, he observed, "What quaint? It's poisonous! You should only know what they put in there."

Startled, Jerry turned abruptly to face the boy as the kid went on with his explanation. "Six ounces a day for a month, and it's goodbye, Charlie."

Grabbing the back of the seat in front of him, Jerry pulled himself to his feet and started to walk away. The people one meets on a bus these days!

But the kid wasn't done with his lecture. "You eat enough of that stuff and you get, uh—"

"Hydrolyzed," the black woman offered.

"Yeah, hydrolyzed—from head to foot!" the boy shouted. Jerry moved away as far as he could. "You'll have yourself a one hundred percent, gung-ho, bananas caterpillar, believe me, mister!"

By this time, everyone on the bus was looking at Jerry as he clung to the overhead bar near the side door. Thinking quickly, he held the microphone in his hand so that it was plainly visible to all around him. "And there's the vitality of New York friends," he said boldly into the mike as he struggled to lower his voice a full octave. "A city where everyone has an opinion. And now over to Hal Crawford in our studios. Take it away, Hal."

Just then, the bus stopped and the rear doors squeaked open. Still into his newscaster character, Jerry did a slow about-face and swaggered across the bus to the doors. Waving grandly to the bewildered commuters and priding himself on having resourcefully gotten out of an uncomfortable predicament once again, he stepped down into the doorway and made the proper exit, four feet from the curb.

II

Macy's was one of New York City's oldest and busiest establishments of its kind. As part of the Big Three (along with Bloomingdale's and Gimbel's), Macy's was always aware of the severe competition for supremacy in such a limited market. Hence, every other month the store held a "once-in-a-lifetime" sale. The newspapers had been squawking about the latest sale for days, and by the time Jerry arrived for work, there was a line of first-day women of all ages and sizes accompanied by a surprising number of children. They huddled against the wall of the building for its entire length—one full city block.

Passing the anxious stream of bargain hunters, Jerry continued to talk into the tape machine. "Okay, kids from five to eight years old have to be sucked into this book in less than fifty words. Let's see—"

The people on line turned to watch as this seemingly average, well-kept man walked by, carrying on a steady conversation with his right hand. A mother near the front door put her arms protectively around her small daughter and drew her close. Unaware of the quizzical stares of the shoppers, Jerry passed the main entrance, waved to the security guard, and proceeded to the service door around the corner. "Uh . . . it was a perfect spring morning. A yellow sun riding a sparkling blue sky, green bursting from every tree and bush . . ."

He arrived at the small door, reached up, and pushed the buzzer. A face appeared in the mirrored window and a return buzzer unlocked the door long enough for Jerry to enter.

"Somehow, the moment Calvin Caterpillar awakened, he knew that today would be different." He was rolling now, and had to get as much on tape as he could before work pulled his attention away from his writing.

The bleak corridor was bustling with its usual pre-sale actvity. Racks of dresses were being scuttled back and forth. Huge cardboard boxes were being emptied of their merchandise and tossed into the mammoth bin near the garage. Men with clipboards hovered over every piece of stock and registered its arrival and departure with some obscure system of checks and double checks.

Coming fully aware of just where he was for the first time, Jerry looked at his watch and groaned. Late again. He clicked off the tape and dropped the mike into his pocket as he ran toward the time clock at the end of the hallway. Taking his punch card from the slot and inserting it into the clock, he hesitated. A thought had struck. Quickly, he pulled out the mike and said, "The name Calvin really—" He plunged the card in all the way. "—stinks." The clock punctuated his displeasure so loudly that Jerry was convinced it was part of some sublime conspiracy to alert the authorities to his tardiness. As if to confirm his theory, Mr. Madden, the shriveled old director of Macy's personnel department, appeared in the doorway.

Grabbing up a large cardboard box and pretending to look busy, Jerry forced his way through the swinging double doors and hurried onto the main floor. Once free of Mr. Madden's scowl, he deposited the box on the cosmetics counter and went to the employees' elevator at the rear of the building beyond Ladies' Foundations. The store would open any minute and he had to rush. As he entered the elevator, he pulled out his name tag, a teddy bear holding a balloon on which was written "Mr. Green." As he absently pinned it to his lapel, he went back to the book he was writing in his mind.

"Why does it all have to alliterate? Forget all names starting with C. Maybe try F. Frank. Fred. Feldman. Feldman? Oh, that's memorable."

The elevator shuddered to a stop and Jerry took a deep breath while the doors slid open. Time to get it together before stepping into what definitely was going to be a tough day. This floor was called Bambini. An entire level of nothing but toys, sporting goods, cribs, children's clothes, magic, dolls, coloring books, etc.; everything that any kid in New York could possibly want was available in Bambini. Macy's prided itself on taking excellent care of the children of its patrons. Today's jumprope purchaser is tomorrow's washing machine customer.

Walking briskly toward his counter, Jerry weaved his way through the busy clerks who were fortifying their defenses against the insane onslaught that waited outside. Thousands of advertisement-crazed buyers chomping at the bit: a vice-president's dream; a salesgirl's nightmare.

Once he had arrived at the glass case and shelves where he would spend the rest of the day, he quickly straightened out the party costumes and accessories that were his domain. Cap pistols hung on pegs and hidious fright masks dangled on strings from the overhead lights. Makeup and disguise kits, false teeth and funny hats all had a specifically-designated space that was computer-determined to aid in efficient sales to the public. Maximum visibility and availability. Any kid would have to have his eyes closed to miss seeing any of this stuff.

After pulling his order book from the drawer and slipping a fresh lead into his mechanical pencil, Jerry leaned back against the clown suit display and spoke softly into the mike.

"Feldman the Caterpillar. I can just see him gorging himself on liverwurst while this demented robin is organizing a pogrom. . . ." He closed his eyes and chuckled at his joke, once again his own best audience.

"You're talking to yourself, Jerry."

Jerry stood upright quickly and whirled toward the voice. Helene stood next to the counter and watched him with quiet amusement. She was a pleasant-looking woman in her mid-twenties. Unspectacular face; absolutely spectacular chest. Well aware of her natural gifts, she was prone to wearing tight, inviting sweaters that revealed every gorgeous curve and delicious bump. Her pastime was watching the other clerks twitch and agonize every time she walked by. Not one for empty promises, she was also prone to end up prone with whomever she fancied. And for the time being, she fancied Jerry. In department store parlance, she had the goods, and delivery was free to preferred customers.

She moistened her lips with the tip of her tongue as she came around the display and approached Jerry. A gold pendant of a bunny rabbit rested comfortably on the ledge provided by her considerable cleavage.

"To some people, that's craziness," she said. "To me, it's a very attractive trait."

"Really?" asked Jerry as he slouched back into the costumes as if seeking a cozy place to hide. "Why?"

Flicking her hand as if to shoo away the question, Helene answered, "That's neither here nor there." She closed the gap between them and fingered Jerry's teddy bear suggestively. Her long wine-hued nails made tiny circles at a spot people don't ordinarily associate with teddy bears. "I called you last night."

"I know." Jerry was now surrounded by clown suits, his back against the cool wall. "I spoke to you, Helene."

She lowered her hand and turned away, moving back to the side of the counter. Jerry, realizing the coast was momentarily clear, emerged from the costume rack and

19

tentatively followed her, keeping his distance. A fish circling the shiny lure.

"That's not the point, she said summoning her lips to purse into her best pout. "*I* called *you*." A curious, hurt, little-girl look came over her face and she turned on her heel. Wiggling in all the right places, she moved to her station at the stuffed animal display. Jerry gave chase.

"That was the entire subject matter of our conversation last night," she said, as Jerry worked his way down the counter, running his hand gently over the soft fluff of the multicolored animals. "Except for the part about lust."

Stopping at the end of the case, Jerry stood eye to eye with an enormous giraffe. "Helene, I haven't got time for lust." He held out his hands in despair. "Hell, I haven't even got time for lunch anymore."

Helene was about to speak, but Jerry threw one arm dramatically around the giraffe's neck and lifted one of its floppy ears. Leaning close, he cooed in a throaty stage whisper, "You're gorgeous. If I could only afford it, I'd set you free."

The giraffe was unresponsive, but Helene was peeved. "Jerry, I'm serious!"

"Why? You're not an endangered species."

Fuming, Helene grabbed the giraffe away from him and tossed it against a bin of tiny koala bears. "No? What about the Thanksgiving Day Parade? Walking next to you, I was practically extinct! You never even talked to me." She began to compulsively rearrange the toys on the countertop. "I mean, if waltzing around in a Winnie the Pooh costume is more important to you than discussing libido deficiencies—"

Jerry reached out and clasped both of her hands in his, trying to calm her down. He could tell when her rage was beginning to build and the last thing he wanted was a full-blown battle scene complete with sound effects, especially with the store opening any second.

"Helene, when Masters and Johnson have a parade, we'll talk about libido deficiencies."

She pulled her hands away and almost shouted back at him. "See how defensive you are?" she said, poking her finger into his badge. "For instance. Why do you worry so much about what you score on the whoopee meter?"

At this, Jerry went pale. The smile he'd been struggling to maintain wilted and he bit the insides of his cheeks in discomfort. Helene noticed that Jerry had suddenly lost his playful mood and she was quick to soothe. She knew him well enough to know that if he wasn't coming back with rapid one-liners, he was retreating into himself. "Hey, it doesn't matter to me— honest." "Yeah, but that's how I was brought up." He allowed his eyes to meet hers. "It comes with the territory." His gaze shifted to the mother lode beneath her sweater. "Uh, strike the word 'territory.' "

"Look, Jerry," she went on, "if I didn't want to go to bed with you, I wouldn't." She smiled and put a hand on his shoulder, softly, without challenge. "How much I enjoy it is my problem."

"Well, I consider how much you enjoy it my problem too."

She squeezed his shoulder. In spite of herself, her hand drifted to his ear and she tickled him under the lobe. "Listen, any time you're ready for another shot at the summit—"

Jerry grabbed her hand and firmly placed it on the back of a large green turtle. "I'm taking you out to dinner tomorrow night. We can talk then."

Warming at the prospect, she smiled and said, "Yes. Some place nice—some place where you have to wear a tie. We agreed on that."

"Right. We'll both wear ties."

A loud bell rang out three times and a nervous hush fell over the floor. Clerks glanced over the goods in their departments one last time, like raw recruits checking their gear before going over the top.

"Gotta run, Helene. You know what that bell means."

She nodded curtly, still angry with him. The near-maniacal hubbub of the once-in-a-lifetime-sale customers grew closer and closer as the escalators hummed to life.

Jerry smiled weakly and fled to man his station.

Downstairs, Cappy, the security guard, had abandoned his post a split second before the bell went off. He'd been through enough of these campaigns and knew better than to be trampled senseless by the hordes of shoppers. At the signal, the velvet rope that provided the flimsy barrier between a cold November morning and the famous Macy's "Penny Pincher" sale was ripped from its stanchion and the main floor was flooded with desperate humanity.

The overflow oozed up the escalators, filled the second-floor clothing, shoe and sleepwear sections in just under two minutes and pressed upward and onward toward *Bambini*.

As the commotion neared, Jerry fiddled with the costume rack. "Maybe it's a girl caterpillar," he mused.

A mannequin in a pirate suit crashed to the floor, twisting one of its arms over its head at a peculiar angle. "Lulu!" A woman's voice scolded harshly. "For God's sake, will you stop that!"

The day had finally begun. Salespeople moved expertly to intercept the first wave of consumers as the bargain hunters engulfed the floor in a matter of seconds. Kids flitted here and there like blips on a radar screen and harried mothers haggled with the already-exhausted staff.

But Jerry was in another world. "Lulu, Lulu," he repeated, feeling the word as it rolled over his tongue. "Lulu the caterpillar shivered in the early morning frost. She knew it was nearly time to spin her cocoon."

A stand of pogo sticks clattered to the floor and brought him back to his senses. Lulu was the wrong name.

"No way," he sniffed. "Lulu the Hooker nailed her first trick of the evening on Eighth Avenue and Fortieth Street and together they—"

Although hundreds of kids and parents swarmed all over the floor like bugs conquering a picnic, Jerry caught the slightest glimpse of one particular woman through the crowd and, for the first time that morning, stopped talking to himself. It was her hair. The first thing he could see clearly as he raised up on his toes was her hair. She was on the other side of the department and a sea of bobbing heads separated them, but Jerry's eyes locked on her and could not be averted. The natural flow of the crowd was carrying her toward him.

The hair. Full, blonde, with a few delicate hints of a darker beige suggested throughout, swirling in healthy, vital waves to her shoulders. As she worked her way closer, Jerry was able to get a better look at the woman beneath the exquisite hair. The glimpse gave way to an out-and-out stare as he stood in reverent appreciation of a truly singular beauty.

Her face was classically drawn. High, proud cheekbones, flawless skin and a tiny, aristocratic nose. Soft lips and perfect teeth that seemed to be illuminated from within. A proper beauty; the girl of any man's dreams. Jerry felt divinely privileged just to be allowed to look for a while and remember this moment forever.

As she wandered through the shoppers, Jerry noticed that, for all her exquisitite appearance and posture, she was dressed rather simply. Washed-out jeans, a pink T-shirt under a blue workshirt tied at the waist. White tennis shoes and no belt. Her only concession to fashion was a navy blue Anne Klein scarf tied loosely around her neck, almost as an afterthought.

When she finally emerged from the milling people, Jerry saw that she was not alone and he sighed. It figured. Not that he had the slightest chance of ever getting to know someone like her, but the ten-second fantasy that had just raced through his mind would have lasted him a couple of months.

She was pushing a stroller toward Helene's counter, and when she got there, she stood by patiently as the baby reached up and ran his wet fingers up and down the legs of the stuffed giraffe. He was about one and a half years old, with soft, dark hair and large, brown eyes. Completely fascinated with all the sights and sounds around him, his attention was drawn back and forth between whatever was brightest or loudest nearby. When Helene tallied a sale and rang the cash register, the baby leaned over alertly to watch.

His mother smiled and reached into the carryall canvas bag that hung on the handle of the stroller. Pulling out a box of Mr. Pretzel fresh-baked pretzels, she came around the side of the carriage and knelt next to her son. After giving the boy a pretzel, which he grabbed at with both hands and devoured, she rose, and as she was about to close the box, it slipped from her fingers and toppled to the floor, spilling pretzels everywhere.

Jerry, of course, had witnessed the whole procedure, but he remained glued to his counter for another few seconds. This was his chance, but he couldn't quite bring himself to believe it yet. This sort of thing just didn't happen to him. Gathering his senses and his courage into one quivering mass, he abandoned his customers and crossed to the lovely woman in less than a second.

Squatting down to scoop up the pretzels at the same instant that she knelt to retrieve them, Jerry kept his mouth shut, not trusting his voice to function at a crucial time like this. He pushed the pretzels around a bit, more like rearranging them than picking them up. Anything to help make the moment linger. She looked over at him, her face only a few inches from his, and smiled.

"Oh. Thank you. I'm sorry . . ."

Jerry gallantly held up his hand and fought for control of his vocal cords. "No problem," he squeaked.

"I hardly ever spill these in stores," she said, picking them up one by one. "It's mostly in the park." Realizing what she had just said, she let out a little laugh that almost knocked Jerry over. "I meant—"

"Honestly, it's no problem," Jerry insisted as they both rose to their feet. "With all the kids coming in here you couldn't begin to imagine what gets on the floor."

They stood facing each other in a deliciously awkward moment, their hands full of pretzels. Then she held her hands over his and let her pretzels fall onto his, creating a huge mound that overflowed back down to the floor.

"It's not unusual for the entire staff to walk out of here at night with lollipops and jelly beans stuck to the bottoms of both shoes," Jerry said, as he helplessly watched a steady stream of salt and crumbs trickle through his fingers.

At this, the young lady threw back her head and laughed heartily, her hair bouncing and teeth sparkling. For a normal shlep like Jerry, it was almost too much to bear. He was thrilled that she had a good enough sense of humor to laugh at his jokes, and he was suddenly quite uncomfortable. He shifted in place for a few seconds, then fled behind Helene's counter to dump the pretzels into a wastebasket. Fighting for his composure, he stole a glance at Helene. Busy with a customer. He was on his own here, all alone in the big time.

Trying to quiet his churning stomach, he came around from behind the giraffe and returned to the stroller just as two plump little boys dressed exactly alike in a nightmare of plaids walked by. Their four fat feet passed over where the pretzels had fallen and they crunched their way noisily toward the elevators.

"There'll be pigeons taking the express up to the third floor tonight," Jerry's new friend said when he reached her side.

Jerry nodded, not ready to trust himself or his voice just yet.

"Thanks very much for helping me," she said as she pulled a tissue from her purse and leaned over her baby.

"Uh, that's okay . . . uh . . ."

But she was busy wiping away the crumbs from her son's face and gently brushing her cheek against his. Jerry stood by quietly and watched as mother and son shared a quiet moment in the middle of all the craziness in the store.

"You're a kind and considerate baby," she cooed, in a soft, tender voice. "And I love you for not calling me 'butterfingers.' " She brushed away the last of the crumbs. "There you go. All better."

"He—I mean, he wouldn't know how to say that— uh, would he?" Jerry asked, as she rose and snapped her purse closed.

She smiled, perhaps patronizing him, perhaps pleasantly. "No."

Jerry shook his head in embarrassment. "No—of course not."

The young lady picked up on his fidgeting and went on to explain. "His two best words so far are 'mama' and 'up.' Everything else comes out sounding like 'egg.' "

"Egg?" Jerry asked, grateful to be standing there and actually having a conversation with this wonderful vision of a woman.

"Yes. You know. Eggeggegg," she said in baby talk. "He loves to say that—and he hates eggs."

"Maybe it's a defense mechanism," Jerry offered, "like inviting your dentist over to dinner."

She laughed again. Then they both laughed. A silence fell over them as they both stopped after laughing a little too long. A silence in the middle of the tumult of a Macy's sale.

Jerry played with his badge and shot a look over to his counter. A line of customers was waiting to be helped and a bunch of kids were systematically destroying the carefully-ordered display. He couldn't care less.

"I don't know very much about babies," he said trying to crank up the conversation again.

"Well," she replied easily, "I'm still learning, myself."

And with that, she slipped her purse over her shoulder, turned the stroller around, and began to walk toward the elevators. "Bye," she smiled.

But Jerry couldn't bear to let this gorgeous creature get away. Not yet anyway. His mind raced for something clever to say, for absolutely anything to say.

"Hey!" he blurted out, stepping forward tentatively. She stopped and turned toward him. He promptly backed off a few steps. "Was there any particular department—" he stammered, "I mean, can I help you with—uh, directing you around?"

"No, thanks," she said. He wilted. "We're just sort of wandering. He likes it better than the zoo." She reached down and ruffled the baby's hair.

"There's a children's barbershop upstairs. You could watch them give haircuts," Jerry said quickly before she could prepare to leave.

Once again, she laughed.

"No, that was crazy." He looked away. "I suppose you're probably headed for the electric trains."

"No. That was last week. I think maybe the Creative Playthings wooden toy set-up." She made the slightest move to turn away.

"There's a terrific display of hockey sticks a few aisles back there on the left—all lined up." Even Jerry knew that his imagination was failing him. Hockey sticks?

"I'll remember that. Thanks." And she started to wheel away again.

He couldn't bear to let her go. "Uh . . . excuse me . . ." She stopped, turned to him and smiled pleasantly, expectantly.

Jerry plunged his hands deep into his pockets and shifted his weight from foot to foot. "I just wanted to—" He was struggling, begging himself to think of something, anything. "I just wondered what his name was," he said at last, nodding toward the child in the stroller.

"Benjamin."

"Benjamin. Right." He straightened his tie for the tenth time since he'd met this woman. "Thanks. He's a sweet baby."

He did an abrupt about-face and scurried back to his display, leaving her and the baby alone in the middle of the floor. She watched him until he plunged into the clump of customers gathered around the rack of costumes, then she wheeled the stroller around and walked away.

Jerry plunked a plastic space helmet onto the head of the little girl who was trying to get it over her ears. Looking over the tops of the heads of the kids who stormed his counter, he watched the most beautiful woman he had ever seen in his life walk away from him.

He knew he'd drive himself crazy thinking about her all day. Settling into his routine of writing orders, accepting checks and slapping tiny hands away from the toy guns, he felt himself slowly turning into a full-fledged, lovestruck basket case.

He wouldn't have had it any other way.

III

Jerry, being a creature of habit, spent every lunch hour at the Museum of Modern Art. Something about its huge, cavernous spaces made him feel secure, isolated, and cozy in a massive world. He, like everyone else in New York, had his own particular favorite sculptures and paintings, but usually he passed the time making notes for his latest book and watching the people stroll about. Often he would just find a spot on some concrete bench in the lobby, close his eyes, and listen. Footsteps echoing hollowly, groups of schoolchildren, organized tours of visitors mumbling in exotic foreign tongues, traffic noise rushing in whenever the doors were opened; this became his private world of safety and familiarity.

On the rare autumn days when the weather was gentle enough to permit it, Jerry would cross through the lobby and spend his hour in the beautiful, open sculpture garden that bordered the rear of the building. This multileveled, tree-lined retreat was a haven for anyone who sought a spot of calm amid the frenzy of a Manhattan business day.

Passing through the tall glass doors and coming into the Garden, Jerry turned to his right and stopped in front of his favorite sculpture, Rodin's statue of Balzac. There the grand, French man of letters stood, elegantly wrapped in a flowing cape. He seemed to peer majestically, almost disdainfully, over the heads of his admirers.

Walking past the glass doors again, Jerry strolled along the imposing panels of nudes that comprised a large portion of the museum's rear wall. Musing over the lovely forms, he continued to his right and ambled down a path lined with low benches. Something caught his eye and he stopped in his tracks.

There, among the many noontime art patrons, was the lady he had met in the store the previous day. She was seated on a bench in the middle of the row, her head thrown back and her face warming in the sun. Her baby, Benjamin, sat in his stroller and quietly watched the pigeons as they bobbed about in search of crumbs, or, better still, a handout.

Jerry's first impulse was to tuck his briefcase up under his arm, turn around, and run away as fast as he could. But he was no fool. Opportunities such as this seldom presented themselves to the Jerry Greens of the world. Throwing caution to the wind and fighting to control his boiling stomach, he strode briskly down the lane.

Staring intently forward as if on some important mission, he walked up to her bench. Then in front of it. Then past it. He stopped and turned around with the air of someone who had forgotten something. He passed the bench again, as slowly as he could. Benjamin looked up for a second, then returned his attention to the birds. His mother continued to sun herself, her lush hair hanging invitingly over the back of the bench.

Realizing that this charade wouldn't work on a woman with her eyes closed, Jerry simply walked to the end of her bench and said, "Hello."

Shading her eyes with her hand, she looked up at him and just stared blankly. Then, when her eyes grew accustomed to the sunlight, she recognized him. "Hello yourself," she said brightly.

"I was just—walking. It's my lunch hour," Jerry explained as he went into his fidgeting routine.

She checked on Benjamin and looked up at Jerry. "It's beautiful out."

"Yeah," he confirmed, "it is." He knelt down and chucked the boy playfully on the chin. "Hey there, Benjamin."

"You remembered his name," she said in pleasant surprise.

"Well, I only met him yesterday," he said as he stood up again.

Inching closer to the edge of the bench, Jerry changed the briefcase from hand to hand. The lady slid over a foot or so, obviously making room for him to join her. Or was she? Perhaps, he thought to himself, she was just trying to slide away from him. He'd just talked himself into another awkward situation.

Seizing the initiative and rubbing his clammy hands against his sweater, he managed to ask, "Is it okay if I sit down?"

She patted the space she had reserved for him and smiled. "Of course."

In a flash, he was seated next to her, briefcase on his lap, hands folded demurely. "Uh, do you come here often?" Someday, he thought, he'd come up with an original line. But this would have to do for now.

"Yeah, pretty much," she said, unzipping her grey sweatshirt. She was wearing a Yankees T-shirt underneath and the same jeans from the day before. "We live near here, so it's easy for us."

"Uh-huh—" And just like that, he was out of things to say again. Think, Jerry, he prodded himself, think. He had it! "Do you mind if I eat my lunch?"

"Well, considering it's your lunch hour, I think you should. By all means."

Jerry now had something to do with his hands, something to occupy his attention for a minute. What a relief. He snapped open the briefcase, removed a yellow legal pad and pulled out a sandwich wrapped in Saran Wrap. Then he closed the case and set it on the ground. Using the legal pad as a lap tray, he set the sandwich down and turned to face his hostess.

"I do this most days, when it isn't raining," he said, as he unwrapped his lunch. "It's a good place to eat if you can develop a fierce look at the moment of unveiling the sandwich."

"Why a fierce look?" she asked.

"To let the pigeons know that they're out of luck," he said, as he contorted his face and stuck out his tongue at the pigeons. Benjamin giggled at the silly man, and the pigeons gathered for a closer look. They were soon joined by sparrows and blackbirds that floated down from the trees all around. No fierce look in the universe ever kept a big-city bird away from Wonder Bread.

Shrugging off the fearless pigons, Jerry took a small bite from his sandwhich and chewed happily. When he shifted to face the lady, he saw that she had been watching him intently the whole time.

"Listen," he said, swallowing hard, "I can't eat this whole thing by myself. Would you like to go halfsies?"

Tucking her leg up under her like a little girl, her face lit up and she said, "Oh God, I'm starving. Do you mean it?"

"Please. Take half," he said. But she had already reached across and plucked half the sandwich from his lap.

In a matter of seconds, most of it was gone as she devoured it in quick tiny bites. "It's marvelous," she said, forcing herself to slow down.

"It's just provolone and anchovies. Most people don't like anchovies." He noticed that she was almost done. "But I guess you don't mind them."

Her mouth was too full to respond, so she just nodded enthusiastically. They sat that way for a few more minutes, she gobbling and he eating slowly.

When they had both finished, Jerry wadded the

Saran Wrap into a ball and tossed it nonchalantly into a trash can a few feet away. He said a silent prayer of gratitude to the great basketball god in the sky and shook the crumbs off the yellow pad.

"Is that your work?" the young lady asked, pointing to the paper.

"Uh-huh," he muttered, and placed it on the bench between them.

"I don't mean to intrude or anything—" she said.

He wanted to yell out: Are you kidding? Intrude! Go ahead, and please intrude! But he just said, "No, no. It's fine. It's just a children's book I'm writing." He struck his author's pose—not unlike Balzac—and waited for her reaction.

It came as expected. "Really?" she asked. "I always wanted to do that—I don't mean write." She uncrossed her legs. "I'd like to do illustrations for children's books."

"Did you ever try?"

"No. I don't draw much anymore. I used to. I went to art school and—" She put her foot on the bottom of Benjamin's stroller and tied her shoe. "Well, anyway. Maybe when the kid here starts school and I have more time."

Tugging at her shoelaces a bit more forcefully than necessary, she proceeded to tie her other shoe as well. Then her hand moved unconsciously to the cord of her sweatshirt hood. Deep in thought, she absently twirled the cord around her finger. Whatever was troubling her seemed to pass and she turned back to Jerry.

"Is this the first one you're writing?" she asked.

"No," he answered in a reserved voice. He'd watched her go through a difficult moment, albeit fleeting, but it had moved him. Shaking it off, he went on to say, "Actually, it's my twenty-ninth."

"Twenty-ninth!" she exclaimed, genuinely impressed. "Would I know your name? Are you famous?"

"Jerry Green. Jerome."

She closed one eye and thought long and hard. "No. I don't think so."

"I've never been published," he confided.

"Oh!" she said and started to laugh. She stopped suddenly and held her fingers to her mouth. "I didn't mean to laugh. That just came out funny."

"I know," he said gently. "I keep submitting them to the publishers and they keep looking at me like 'what is this nonsense you're bludgeoning us with.' It's like saturation bombing. Only it's twenty-nine misses and not one hit." He took the legal pad and held it out in front of him as if hoping to find what was wrong with his writing.

"Maybe it's because I can't write down to little kids. For instance—" He suddenly lowered the pages and felt very self-conscious. "Am I talking too much?"

"No, of course you're not," she said soothingly. "Honestly."

He patted the paper and said, "The one I'm writing now is about a caterpillar who worries about the ecology. But I guess that's wrong for kids today."

"No, it's not," she said. "I think it's lovely." Leaning forward, she took an old envelope and a pencil from her purse that hung from the stroller. Flattening out the envelope across her knee, she began to doodle as Jerry spoke.

"Well, he should probably be worrying about what color he's going to be when he becomes a butterfly." His eyes brightened as he spoke. He was in his element, talking about what he loved most. "You see, if he's plain brown, he'll drop dead from embarrassment. But some simpering flower, Gladys Gladiolus—" They both groaned at the name, "—tells him that she won't have any of those gaudy numbers fooling around her pistils and plain brown is beautiful."

He looked over at her, but she was involved with her sketching. "The publishers would eat it up in a second," he went on. "But I just can't write like that."

Pausing to erase a couple of lines, she glanced at him. "Well, I sure couldn't read it," she laughed. "Gladys Gladiolus would probably have a round face with long eyelashes—"

"Right! And no nose."

"Positively no nose for Gladys." She held the pencil sideways and moved it rapidly in delicate swirling circles as she colored in her drawing. "What's your caterpillar's name?"

"Funny you should ask," Jerry said, as he tried to sneak a peek at her work. "I spent my whole lunch hour yesterday working on that."

She looked up for a beat, then went back to putting the finishing touches on her masterpiece. "If it's Fuzzy-Wuzzy, I'll have to ask you to move on."

Jerry watched her for a few seconds, measuring his words. Not wanting to offend his new friend. "It's—Benjamin."

She turned to him and smiled warmly. "Is it really?"

"Yes."

Nudging the stroller with her toe, she asked, "For this Benjamin?"

"Yeah. For your Benjamin."

Her smile broadened and she tilted her head as her eyes twinkled with delight. "That's terrific! We're honored." She pinched the baby on the cheek. "Aren't we, honey?"

Benjamin responded by drooling onto his jacket.

Jerry laughed at the boy's gesture of appreciation and went on to explain, "I thought about it a lot last night. After I—After I saw you in the store." He winked at Benjamin. "It's a good name, kid."

"You're right. It is a good name. I'm glad you picked it." Then she held the sketch out for Jerry to see. "How do you like him?"

Taking the envelope from her, Jerry studied it carefully. A plump, furry caterpillar with a bright, cherubic face was inching along a twig.

"Hey, I like this a lot!" Jerry said earnestly. "He's almost the exaet caterpillar I visualized."

"Why almost?" she asked, her lips betraying the slightest trace of a pout.

"Well, mine is thinner," he was quick to explain. "But you don't know the story." Jerry pulled his heel up onto the edge of the bench and wrapped both his arms around his knee. "You see," he went on, "the caterpillar won't eat leaves, what with the ecology problem and everything. But that's just—" He looked at the picture again. "Listen, this is really good. I love it!"

She smiled shyly, finding it difficult to deal with such a straightforward compliment. "You can have it if you want."

"Thanks. But only if you sign it for me."

"Okay." She took the sketch back and wrote her name across the bottom.

"You should really put together some drawings and take them to the children's book publishers. I really think you—" Just then she handed him the envelope and he stopped to read her name. "—Jenny Moore—"

He caught her eyes with his and said, "Jenny Moore—You have a lot of talent."

She pulled her gaze away and it was her turn to fidget. "Thanks. I'm not—uh, you have to be in the right mood in order to—" Jenny seemed to feel uneasy, not quite sure of her thoughts.

Trying to bring the conversation back around to some sort of even keel, Jerry pointed to Benjamin and asked, "He's your baby. I mean, your own natural-born son, right?"

"Yeah."

"And that's probably your wedding ring, there, right?

"Right again."

Jerry picked up his briefcase and slipped the legal pad inside. "So this whole conversation is out of the question." He snapped the case shut. "That's not what I meant to say. It's—uh . . ."

36

He was in trouble and she came to the rescue. "Why? We exhanged gifts of food as is written in the ancient books. So now we're friends."

Jerry dismissed this notion with a shrug. "Cheese and anchovies isn't exactly honey and almonds."

"Oh no?" Jenny asked, a hint of mischief floating on her voice. "I wish you hadn't eaten the other half of the sandwich."

Jerry sighed long and hard as he bit his lip and tried to figure out how best to say what was on his mind. Finally, he found himself saying, "Well, I wish you were just the babysitter, not the mommy."

Just as Jenny was about to answer, Jerry stood up impulsively and prepared to leave. "I have to go. Thanks for the drawing. I probably talked too much." He knew he was talking too much, but he couldn't turn it off.

Jenny looked at him seriously. "No, you didn't. In fact, if anything, *I* was the one—"

But Jerry was backing away. "Goodbye. Thanks a lot for the sketch," he said, holding his briefcase in front of him with both hands.

"Goodbye, Benjamin. Goodbye."

After shuffling backward for a few more steps, he turned and started up the path.

"Goodbye," Jenny called to him, in a voice as sweet as honey and almonds.

Looking over his shoulder, Jerry saw Jenny squatting next to Benjamin. She had the baby's hand in hers and she was helping him wave bye-bye. A strange, exhilirating chill swept through his body as he waved back to them once more and turned to walk away.

His mind was completely out of control and his body was weak. He moved slowly down the lane, hoping to get out of the garden without falling over his own feet or walking into a wall or something.

IV

Later that afternoon, Jerry's mind was into anything but work. But his body had to be there, and he, as a dedicated Macy's employee of many months, carried out his duties with exemplary professional dedication. In the hours that had passed since his fortuitous lunchtime rendezvous with Jenny, he had undercharged tow women nearly one hundred dollars and helped another to her car five blocks away. If pressed, he would have denied that the fact that all three were blonde had had anything to do with it. The first incident was merely an oversight; the second was the least he could do in the name of good service.

The teeming crowds had not diminished some eight hours into the sale. On the contrary, they seemed to be reinforced by some unseen reservoir of humanity that sent a constant flow of new troops into the bargain battles.

Jerry stood behind his counter and did his best to remain upright. Weariness had long since yielded to exhaustion, and by the time the well-dressed, middle-aged couple approached him, he had been running on automatic pilot for nearly two and a half hours.

The man puffed and chewed furiously on a fat cigar. The breast of his expensive beige trenchcoat had long ago been discolored to a sooty grey from too many ashes fallen from too many fat cigars. His wife was meticulously attired in a slinky, green, Bloomingdale's jumpsuit. Neither she nor her husband cared that she was eighty pounds too heavy for that style and that one woman's slink was another woman's slump. It was *de rigueur*. All the other girls had one, so it was her duty to own one as well—even if it made her walk funny.

Taking the cigar from his mouth and flicking a huge ash onto the floor and his left shoe, the man laid a large package down on the counter and said to Jerry, "Write it up. We're in a hurry."

"Right away, sir," Jerry answered, waving the heavy cigar smoke out of his immediate environment. He flipped the box over expertly and noted the stock numbers. Then he tallied the price and tax, and wrote out a purchase slip. As he was about to slide the box into a Macy's bag, he noticed the illustration on the cover. The couple was buying a ballerina costume. Pink and white and child-size.

"Are you going to take this with you, or shall I send it over for wrapping?" Jerry asked, trying his best to do a decent job and get out of there on time for once. He had promised to take Helene to dinner that night and he dreaded the thought of not only dealing with her, but just staying awake after six o'clock.

"We'll take it with us, thank you," the man said as he absently brushed at his coat.

The woman pulled and tugged at the crotch of her jumpsuit and said, "I still think we should get a larger size."

"Why?" her husband asked. "It's a size eleven. He's eleven. For once something will fit him."

Jerry finished taping the receipt to the bag and tried to play what he'd just heard over again in his mind. He knew he was tired, but not that tired. Sliding the package across the counter, he smiled his thanks and tried to keep a straight face.

"He'll outgrow it in six months," the wife said.

Jerry held onto the package. He wanted to hear more of this.

"So we'll buy him a new one!" her husband snapped. He threw his cigar down and stomped it to bits with his heel. Another customer who was looking at rubber knives right next to him had to retreat a few steps to escape having his right foot mistaken for a cigar butt and being crushed into tiny pieces.

"Isn't that what being rich is all about?" the man continued. Then he leaned across the countertop and blasted Jerry with a stream breath as he demanded, "This is for a normal eleven-year-old child, isn't it?" He smashed the package with the palm of his hand and the top of the box caved in.

Trying to breathe out of the corner of his mouth and still speak straightforwardly, Jerry mumbled, "Well . . . in terms of length . . . the tutu will fit . . . uh, him . . . right about here." And he stepped back to indicate a point on his upper thigh. Then he put his hands above his belt and went on, "Now, around the waist—" He couldn't believe this was happening. Braving the demonic breath of the angry man, he ventured closer and said, "Actually, you should know that this is a ballerina costume."

Having said this, he looked from the man to the woman and back to the man for some reaction. Nothing doing. Then he pulled the box out of the bag and pointed to the picture of a sweet little girl in a frail tutu standing on pointed toes.

"There's the picture right there. A ballerina."

"What about the waist?" the husband asked, not about to have his attention diverted. He assumed that everyone knew that rich people can buy whatever they damn well pleased, and no questions asked.

Jerry threw the gender lesson aside and played it straight. "He may have to cut down on sweets, but that's a minor—"

By this time, the wife, who had been steaming on a

40

slow boil, finally had heard enough of this clerk's nonsense and her husband's tirades. "Okay! Just put it back into the bag!" She grabbed the package and shoved it into her husband's arms. "For Christ's sake, let's get out of here. I'm hungry."

With that, she pulled on her husband's sleeve and the two of them stalked away.

Jerry tried not to look at her ponderous behind as it struggled to get free of the confines of the jumpsuit. But, being normal and incurably nosy, he stared after them until they rounded the corner at the camping display.

Once they had passed from sight, he moved over to wait on the customer who had been looking at the fake daggers. "May I help you, sir?" he asked brightly.

"Why, yes," the man said, laying the knife back into its tray. "I'm interested in trying on that Alice in Wonderland outfit you have advertised."

V

The newest restaurant sensation on the East Side, the Kitsch Inn, was doing its usual landslide business that evening. Since it had been reviewed in *New York* magazine, it had gone from a marginally unsuccessful family venture to a dynamic, swinging nightspot. Just another overnight success that had been in the neighboorhood for fifteen years.

Once the crowds had discovered the Kitsch Inn, the owners bought the flower shop next door, knocked out the wall, and squeezed enough tables to accomodate another two hundred diners. Then came the obligatory Boston ferns and rattan ceiling fans. Wicker chairs and a copper and mahogany bar followed soon after, and a quiet dining room was transformed into a Manhattan mayhem muncherie.

The beautiful people had been packing the place nightly for months. Young lawyers and advertising executives tried their routines on sweet, swinging secretaries who had heard it all before over frozen daiquiries. Tweedy young women execs with money to burn put the moves on nervous network and magazine hotshots and either took them home with them or dumped them after one boring drink.

It was a "scene" of the first degree, and these people thrived on being part of the scene. They hopped from table to table, chattering loosely about conquests, real and imagined. Service here was notoriously bad, and the customers were equally renowned for being big tippers. Plans were in the works for opening another Kitsch Inn in Los Angeles, and franchise inquiries had been coming in from Chicago, New Orleans, and Seattle. The place was a madhouse from opening bell to last call. A madhouse and a gold mine.

It was also Helene's favorite restaurant.

She and Jerry sat scrunched up against the wall at a table that was too small to be a nightstand in a child's room. Munching sloppily on a creamed-chicken crepe while her escort gingerly tried to figure out the secret of his artichoke, she was talking a mile a minute.

"We have different ideas about the function of marriage, that's all," she said as she licked some sauce off the back of her fork. "Mine are normal and you're still in the nineteenth century."

Jerry tugged at a stubborn artichoke leaf. "Why? What did they do then? I can't remember."

"See? That's a typical answer." She pushed a piece of french bread around on the plate. "I'm talking about the sexual favors granted in exchange for concessions of supremacy."

Rather than starve to death, Jerry took his steak knife and hacked away at the artichoke. "Helene, did you ever try to concentrate while you're being attacked by an artichoke?" He placed a leaf in his mouth and scraped off the meat. Chewing slowly, perhaps knowing that he should savor whatever he could get from this vegetable, he asked, "What sexual favors?"

Helen's eyes widened in anger as she tore off a piece of crusty bread and stuffed it into her mouth. "Jerry!" she shouted, sending a fine spray of crumbs his way. "What I'm saying is, I'd marry you under the right conditions. You hear me? Marry!"

Picking a few crumbs off his tie, and working hard at not passing out, Jerry said, "We never talked about marriage before—under any conditions. Don't you see?

43

That was one of the conditions." He methodically stabbed away at his artichoke as he spoke. "Healthy companionship and occasional lust—or occasional companionship and healthy lust. I don't know what the hell you said, but *you* said it, believe me!"

Turning away from her, he folded his arms across his chest and slumped back in his seat. When he looked across the room, his eyes bulged wide and he suddenly got that upside-down feeling in his stomach again. Jenny. Too good to be true, he thought. Jerry blinked twice and looked again. No doubt about it. Jenny.

Jenny Moore was standing at the headwaiter's desk with her husband, Preston. He was a tall, athletic forty-year-old with a head full of thick black hair and a strong, pedigreed jawline. Both of them were dressed elegantly, she in a flowing, white silk pantsuit with a peach shawl, and he in a Pierre Cardin three-piece suit. From where Jerry sat with his mouth fallen open, it appeared that Warren was having some problem with the host. But that was soon remedied with a palmed ten-dollar bill, and an available table was found in a flash.

Even the other women in the restaurant turned to eye Jenny's extraordinary beauty as the headwaiter took up two oversized menus and gestured for the couple to follow him. Taking his wife's arm, Preston guided her across the room—nodding greetings to a few acquaintances along the way—to a booth on the wall opposite Jerry and Helene.

Preston seemed chipper, in his milieu. But Jenny looked utterly miserable. They were just about to be seated when Helene shot Jerry an elbow in the ribs and said, "I'm talking to you!" He looked her way and she went on. "*I'm* interested in a more permanent relationship."

Jerry continued to look at her blankly, not seeing. Then he shifted his gaze back to Jenny. Helene grew furious and shouted, "Jerry!"

At this, the tables in their immediate vicinity became

strangely subdued, the diners straining to hear what had the makings of a good public squabble. Jenny also heard Helene's shout, and turned to see what was happening. Jerry, who was still staring at her, caught her eyes with his and began to rise. But she quickly shook her head, turned away, and allowed the waiter to assist her into the booth.

Helene had taken all of this in, the eye contact between Jerry and the other woman, but she continued with her diatribe. "If we both understand that we're emotionally unstable to begin with—you could even use the word 'crippled' if you want—then maybe we've really got something going." Jerry hardly moved. He wasn't even insulted by her "crippled" remark. "Hey, what's the matter with you, anyway?"

"Nothing," he said as he turned to face her again. "I don't mean to sound flippant, Helene, but you're full of shit."

She was on her feet in less than a second, flames of fury burning in her every word as she slammed her napkin down on the table. "You see what I mean about crippled?" Fumbling to get her purse open in her rage, she knocked over her daiquiri and a light green stain spread across the table cloth.

"Okay, Mr. Smartass! That disgusting chicken pancake cost four-fifty." She threw five dollars at him.

Half-rising from his seat, Jerry reached out for her hand, but she pulled away. "Helene, for crying out loud, I didn't mean to——"

"Keep the change," Helene said icily, her breasts heaving as she struggled to control her temper.

"Look, we can start negotiating for an apology," Jerry said contritely, trying to keep her calm and relatively quiet. "I'll go steadily with you and——"

By this time, Helene had managed to get out from behind the table. "No, thanks," she said, cutting him short. "You just concentrate on that vinaigrette fly trap

45

there—because one mistake, and you're in the Bellevue choke ward!"

Grabbing her sweater from the seat and clutching it roughly in her hand, she stomped across the room and headed for the door. The going slowed considerably when she got to the crowded bar area. Once the young studs got an eyeful of her remarkable chest, they closed in on her in a single-minded, crush, fiends in search of a cheap feel. But Helene was up to the task. She burst through the mob like a fullback and slammed out the revolving door. Two guys gulped their drinks and followed.

Sinking as far as he could into his seat, Jerry watched helplessly as Helene stormed away. Now that the battle was over, the other diners returned to their meals and the chatter picked up again as they fell back into their lively, if empty, conversations. When he turned to look across at Jenny, he hoped she had somehow missed the vitriolic scene. But as soon as their eyes met, he knew she had witnessed the whole ridiculous affair. What could he do? Shrugging pitifully toward her, he sipped at his wine and prepared to drown his sorrows in Zinfandel.

The waiter was taking the dinner order and Warren turned to Jenny to ask, "What kind of dressing do you want?"

"Roquefort," she said hollowly, her thoughts elsewhere.

"Two roqueforts," the waiter said and, with a slight bow, he headed for the kitchen.

Jenny was still looking across to Jerry who was somewhere in the middle of his second glass of wine. Jerry looked up and saw that she was watching. The embarrassment of the fiasco disappeared as soon as Jenny smiled.

"What's wrong?" Preston asked of his wife as he

46

peered around the room to spot whatever had captured her interest.

"Oh—" she began emptily. Then she turned to him and said, "Nothing."

"Good. Are you hungry?"

"Sort of, I guess."

Breaking a roll apart with his hands, Preston munched away as he spoke. "I'm starving. I had a hell of a day today. No lunch. I had to cancel the squash game, I didn't get my haircut, and I had eight separate, very boring meetings." He reached across the table for the butter. "I'm really bushed. So I'm just going to eat, take a shower, and go to sleep."

Just like every night, Jenny thought, as she smiled shallowly at her husband. Then she rose up a little in her seat to see how Jerry was doing. He was still working on the wine.

Preston shifted around and looked impatiently for the waiter. "I'm playing squash tomorrow instead," he continued. "I'll probably get killed. It's some new member who's supposed to be dynamite." Seeing that his wife was still staring off into space, he put his hand on hers and squeezed until she turned to face him.

"Jenny, you're not listening to me."

She pulled her hand from his and busied herself with the drinks the waiter was just setting down. "Yes I am, dear," she said as she sipped at her Coke. "What happened at your eight separate boring meetings?"

"Nothing spectacular," Preston said feigning humility as he took the olive from his very dry vodka martini. "I was quietly brilliant in seven of them and I reamed out that Harvey Nicholson in the eighth."

"Why?" Jenny asked automatically. They were going through their daily motions which consisted of Warren talking about himself and Jenny persuading her mind not too wander off too far.

"Because it seemed to be the right thing to do. And it turned out that it was." He tossed back half his martini.

47

"First drink today," he said. "By the way, we're invited to the Barkers' for the weekend. In the company jet."

"Oh? All because you reamed out that Harvey Nicholson?" Jenny was surprised at her own bitchy behavior, but she let it stand.

Preston, however, was growing annoyed by his wife's manners. But he was a man of quiet control and he fought to maintain his composure. "No, because Barker considers me promising partner material. That's why."

"What do we do with Benjamin if we go away?" she asked.

"We'll have Flora stay with him. It's only a weekend. It'll be good for you to get away from him for a few days." He waited until she looked at him before going on. "And I'll tell you something else; it'll be good for him too."

"Teach him a little self-reliance at eighteen months?" Jenny asked, the sarcasm creeping into her voice.

"What's wrong with that?" her husband demanded as he buttered his second piece of bread. "In California they've got kids who can swim by the time they're Benjamin's age."

Jenny pushed her Coke away and stared at her hands. "Right. I forgot about that," she said, her voice barely audible above the din of the supper crowd.

Preston's minimal patience was stretched about as far as it would go. "What the hell's the matter with you?"

"Nothing," she responded mechanically.

"Did something happen today?"

"No," Jenny said as she shook her head. "We just went to the museum." Pulling a wisp of hair away from her eyes, she turned to him and tried her best to converse with him in a civil manner. "Benjamin discovered that Play-doh is too drab for his sophisticated taste."

"Why do you let him put things like that in his mouth?"

"Because he wants to. He's experimenting with everything he can get his hands on. It's good for him."

The level of tension at their booth heightened markedly and the same diners who had quieted down in order to hear Jerry and Helene now hushed their own jabber to better hear Jenny and Preston. It sounded like it might get out of hand and they were delighted.

"Well, eating Playdoh *isn't* good for him," Preston asserted. "It's pointless."

It was becoming increasingly difficult for even the false levity to remain in her voice. "It really isn't pointless, dear. It's how he learns."

"How he learns what?"

By this time the bus boy was making it a point to come to their table as often as possible so that he could get an earful of this spat. He filled their brimming water glasses and emptied their unused ashtray several times as he visited the booth every few minutes.

Jenny blew out a long, controlled breath between clenched teeth. "How he learns that he *can* learn."

This sort of statement and its inherent logic meant nothing to Preston who had a completely different philosophy about child rearing. "All you have to do is tell him what he can do and what he can't do," he said with finality. "That's how kids learn."

Jenny wasn't about to buy this line of reasoning. Not in the mood she was in. Raising her right eyebrow and closing her left eye as if she were supporting a monocle, she said in a thick Gestapo border guard accent, "He *vill* obey orders."

"The hell with it, Jenny!" Preston shouted. The people nearby grinned at each other stupidly in embarrassed reaction to this outburst. "I don't want to talk about bringing up baby tonight. Okay?"

"Okay."

The two of them settled into that middle ground of truce that couples develop. The DMZ where they can send their anger and their hurt feelings and still maintain the delicate status quo.

Preston was the first to speak. "I finally hired a new secretary. He started today."

"Good," Jenny said, still looking across to Jerry who sat against the far wall looking back at her.

"You didn't pick up on the 'he,' " Warren said lightly "It's a man."

"I'm sorry, Preston," she said as she pulled her eyes away from Jerry and turned to her husband. "I did notice that. I should have said something."

"I'm convinced it's a lot more prestigious to have a male secretary. It impresses the clients and enhances my status with the company." He moved his drink to one side to make room for the shrimp cocktails their waiter was about to set down. "I mean there's no question about that."

"Uh-huh. Sort of like getting the key to the executive men's room," his wife taunted. Her water glass was empty. The busboy hadn't even been close to their table since they had stopped quarrelling.

Preston had had enough of this sparring, and Jenny's last barb was too much. "Goddammit! What the hell is wrong with you?" Their water was refilled and the ashtrays were emptied in a matter of moments.

Jenny poked listlessly at her shrimp cocktail for a minute. Then she laid the tiny fork down and dabbed at her lips with her napkin. "I suddenly don't feel—could we go home?"

But Preston wanted to get to the bottom of it and he was not about to be denied. "You suddenly don't feel what?"

"Like staying here," she said, her eyes brimming with tears. "Can't we just leave?"

Before she could get up, Preston grabbed her wrist and shook her arm. "Jenny, I'm tired and hungry," he said in his steely voice. "And I'm going to eat my dinner. Is that understood?"

Allowing her hand to go limp in his, Jenny simply said, "Then would you mind if *I* just—"

50

She didn't have to finish. Preston pushed her hand away and picked up his fork. "No! I wouldn't mind at all. Do what you want."

"I'm sorry," Jenny said as she pulled her shawl over her shoulders. "I'll see you at home. All right?" The bus boy was at the next table. He and the two couples there leaned in to hear Preston's answer.

"That's fine," Preston answered as he dug into the appetizer. His neighbors were disappointed that they weren't going to get a fireworks sideshow that evening and they asked for their check.

Jenny stood there helplessly for a minute, frustrated and at a loss. Then she whirled around and made her way to the door. The young bucks at the bar saw her coming a mile away and they were ready. But once they got a glimpse of the fury in her eyes, they prudently backed off and let her pass.

Jerry had been a silent witness to the whole skirmish, and as soon as he saw that Jenny was actually going to leave, he jumped up and followed her. Grabbing a bunch of flowers from a nearby empty table, he nudged his way through the boozers at the bar and found himself right in the middle of a party of ten that was just coming in for a late dinner.

He turned his body sideways and slithered the last few feet to the revolving door. Once there, he plunged in and was hurtled outside. Narrowly missing the two mashers who had gone after Helene, Jerry found himself standing on the sidewalk looking frantically for Jenny. He gestured to the other guys for help, for any indication, but it was every man for himself as far as they were concerned. Laughing at his plight, they pushed their way back into the restaurant and left Jerry standing there, the bunch of fresh flowers hanging loosely at his side.

Out of the corner of his eye, he spotted her just as she turned the corner at the liquor store and headed across town. Jerry hesitated. If she caught a cab or had a car parked on the street, she would be gone forever. But if he pursued her, she might well be offended. Perhaps she wanted to be alone, to walk the dark, lonely streets in angry solitude. Or maybe she needed a friend. If he stood there any longer trying to come up with excuses, he told himself, he'd freeze to death and she'd be halfway to Detroit.

After glancing back inside the restaurant to make sure that her husband was still at his table, Jerry dashed for the corner. When he got to the liquor store and looked up the side street, he saw that Jenny was almost to the end of the next block. Coins jingling in his pocket and necktie flapping in the wind, he gave chase.

Jenny heard the footsteps coming at her from behind and quickened her pace. When she reached Fifth Avenue, she turned right and walked briskly uptown. Skidding around the corner on one foot, Jerry raced after her. Once he got within a few feet, he slowed to a walk and tried to overtake her. But she was moving too fast and he had to shift into high gear again until he came up beside her.

Fighting to catch his breath, he said, "Hello," and gulped in gallons of oxygen until his heart stopped pounding. He really wasn't in the greatest of shape since he had given up jogging that quarter of a mile every day.

Jenny stopped walking and caught Jerry by surprise. He went on another few feet, and after realizing he was walking alone, came back to her. She stood with her back against the smooth wall of Tiffany's, the cool fluorescent lighting of the window display providing a delicate backlight for her hair and face. The effect was angelic.

"Hello yourself," she smiled, the anger already gone.

But she was so wound up that she had to keep moving. As she started walking again, at a much more leisurely pace this time, Jerry fell into step.

"Are you okay?" he asked.

"Uh-huh."

"Listen. That girl I was with, we have a mutually destructive relationship." Without knowing precisely why, Jerry felt compelled to explain about Helene. "We sort of—disagreed on life just now. At least I think we did. I'm not so sure because I wasn't listening."

He slowed for a second as he reflected upon what had happened earlier. Then he hastened to catch up with Jenny as she reached 57th Street and started to cross Fifth Avenue. "Without being cruel," he continued, "I'm just as glad she left. I just didn't want to spend another evening—"

Jenny had picked up the pace again and didn't seem to be paying any attention to him. Jerry began to feel like a schoolboy chasing after the pretty cheerleader. "Would you rather be alone?" he asked in a small voice.

She stopped in front of Bergdorf-Goodman's and turned to face him. Jerry almost melted under her scrutiny and when she finally smiled, her eyes moist from the cold night breeze, he knew that all was well in the world. At least for the moment.

"No," she said gently. "I'd rather not be alone." She reached across the space between them and took the flowers from Jerry's hand.

Turning to walk up Fifth Avenue again, she held the small bouquet to her nose and moved noticeably slower.

Jerry was flabbergasted and began to chatter nervously. "She's—the girl back there—spectacularly aggressive. Sort of like Hitler poised on the Polish border. Y'know?"

"Uh-huh."

"Anyway, she thinks you can just agree to discuss the inner meaning of life and have it come out right." They waited for a yellow cab to round the corner of 58th Street, then they crossed and headed for the fountain in front of the Plaza Hotel. A few other people strolled quietly and a cluster of pigeons scattered as they approached.

"Well, that's crazy," Jerry rambled on, feeling the need to keep talking. "Or maybe this whole thing is kind of heavy for you, considering you just left your husband back there in the restaurant."

Lifting a white carnation from the flowers in her hand, Jenny sniffed it lightly and tossed it into the churning waters of the fountain. She watched it float and bob for a few seconds before sitting down on the low ledge and looking up to Jerry.

"You're a very nice man," she said.

This shut him up. He smiled weakly, walked in a tight, uneasy circle, and sat down next to her. "I don't know how to respond to that."

"You could agree," she said. She looped her arm through his and snuggled closer.

"Nobody ever said those exact words to me before," he said, loving the magic of the nearness of this marvelous woman. "Okay, I agree." He held up his finger in mock warning. "But only tentatively."

Jenny squeezed even closer and pressed against his arm. They sat like that for a minute or so and watched the horse-and-carriage teams line up across the street at Central Park, waiting for young lovers.

Snuffling his face into her hair, Jerry pulled his arm free and put it around her shoulder. "If this hadn't happened tonight, I was going to try to find your number in the phone book. I think I would have called you, too. I know I would have lurked around the museum a lot."

But this couldn't be true, he thought. This woman, the beautiful Jenny Moore, could not be alone at the Plaza Fountain cuddling with Jerry Green, unpublished author of twenty-nine children's books.

He was suddenly very disturbed by the awesome improbability of the situation. "Look, maybe I should just get you a taxi and forget that your name is Jenny Moore, and then I'll—"

But she pulled away and touched his cheek with her fingertips. "Please don't," she whispered.

"That was your husband back there, wasn't it?" Jerry asked. After she nodded, he went on to say, "I was watching you. You weren't fighting."

"No," she said turning to watch the parade of limousines in front of the Plaza Hotel. "We don't fight."

"How can you be married and not fight?" Jerry asked, inching closer so that her hair brushed against his face again. "That's sort of built into the concept, isn't it?" She shrugged and he continued. "It's supposed to be healthy. I don't mean you should go at each other with tire chains, or—"

Jenny leaned backward into Jerry's arms and lifted her face to look at him. "We don't think it's worthwhile anymore."

"What a sad thing to say," Jerry said as he put his arms around her waist. "I'd consider it extremely worthwhile to—no, that's coming out wrong, too."

"No, it isn't." Jenny put her hands over his and tilted her head back to gaze at the sky.

Jerry continued to hold on to her, praying that this dream would never end. Across the street, two couples climbed into a horse-drawn carriage and clipclopped away.

"I could fall in love with you so fast," he said into her hair. "I'll prove it—I already have."

Shifting around on the ledge, Jenny pulled away from him and maneuvered her body so that they were now hugging face to face. Their cheeks touched and Jerry could feel her breathing against his ear.

Mustering courage he never knew he had, he brought himself to ask, "Can I kiss you?"

In response, Jenny turned her head and kissed him lightly on the nose.

They sat and looked at each other for a few seconds; Jerry still felt the tingle of her touch. "I don't want to press my luck," he said, "but that wasn't what you'd call a real friendly kiss, was it?"

She was about to answer, but he held up his hand. "Wait. I don't have to analyze everything all at once. I mean, how can I speculate on whether or not you have an unhappy marriage just because you walked out of a restaurant?" He took her hand. "Have you?"

"Have I what?"

"An unhappy marriage."

Jenny freed her hand and picked at the flowers in her lap. After a while she said, "Yes," and bit her lower lip pensively.

Jerry put his hand on her shoulder, trying to comfort her and untangle his own thoughts at the same time. "I don't know how to respond to that. Do I say I'm sorry, or tell you I'm glad?"

"You don't have to say anything," she replied, and she pulled her shawl high up on her shoulders.

Intrigued, Jerry leaned close to her and reached out to hold her head in his hands. This woman enchanted him. He squeezed her thick hair and marveled at how uncomplicated and honest she was.

Imperceptibly at first, and then with a bit more purpose, they felt themselves being drawn together by some undeniable passionate magnetic force. Their eyes met and flickered for an instant—each asking, each needing—and then they kissed. Softly at first; new lips exploring, tasting. But soon they melted together and joined in a long urgent, delicious kiss.

"Jenjamin, my love!" came the voice out of the night. Loud and strong. So loud, in fact, that Jerry almost shrieked in fright as he gasped and pulled away from Jenny. He clutched at his heart, as if to keep it from bursting out from beneath his coat, and looked around guiltily.

Jenny turned to see Ernest Van Santen standing on the front steps of the Plaza. He was leaning casually on his walking stick and pulling a pair of fine beige leather gloves out of his magnificent fox-fur coat. A hat tilted at a roguish angle and a white silk scarf completed the outfit. The man presented quite a striking figure of opulence and good taste. Not bad for a man pushing fifty.

He crossed the street and made his way toward the fountain. "How's Benjamin?" he asked congenially.

Jenny nodded pleasantly and said, "He's fine, thanks."

"Marvelous!" he said vigorously as he blew her a kiss and continued on his way, gaily tapping his silver-tipped walking stick as he headed for the Park.

"Uh—" Jerry began, trying to keep his voice from cracking. "Uh, who's that?"

"He and his wife are good friends of ours," she answered, seeming to be unconcerned by the encounter.

"What did he call you? Jenjamin?"

"Yeah," she replied. "A cross between my name and Benjamin's. Just a silly endearment."

"Well, he sounds like he talks in typographical errors. How do you know a guy like that?"

"He lives in our building."

Jerry pulled at his hair, terrified at having been found in such a compromising position. "Oh, that's real helpful."

"He won't say anything," Jenny said, patting his knee. "It'll amuse him not to."

Jerry took a couple of deep breaths and looked at her. She was completely unflustered by the entire affair. Her composure affected him and he came back to earth. "We just had our first fight," he said. "And I don't even know your husband's name."

Reaching up and touching his cheek, Jenny shook her head. "No, we didn't." She smiled. "And it's Preston."

"Preston. *That* I never would have guessed." Jerry nodded toward the dim figure of Van Santen, far away now. "Just suppose he does tell ol' Preston—"

"Well, then," Jenny shrugged, "we can't help that, can we?"

"I love you," Jerry said impulsively. He didn't know he was going to say it and he wasn't even aware he had said it until he heard it himself. "Wait. Don't say anything. I have to figure out how to handle that myself—" Jenny sat back and waited, amused and enchanted.

Jerry looked after Van Santen again, then turned to look at the hotel. Nobody looked back. At that moment, they were the only two people in the world. "I wish you'd say something," he said.

She squeezed his hand and asked, "Do you work on Sundays?"

"Nope."

"Well, I can be here at two o'clock," she said. "Can you?"

Jerry was stunned. There was no way he would ever be able to answer her. He could only nod. He smiled and nodded again, stricken by an incapacitating love-bolt that rendered him speechless and quaking in his penny loafers. He nodded once more.

Jenny laughed and kissed him, a tender peck on the cheek. Then she fluffed up her hair with her fingers and gathered her shawl about her. "Good night. Thanks for the flowers," she said as she rose and made her way toward the corner of Central Park South.

By the time she reached the curb, Jerry was just coaxing his body to react. He stood up numbly and called out, "Hey!"

Stopping at the curb, Jenny turned to face him.

"Good night yourself," he said, and waved.

Jenny waved back as the light turned green. She walked briskly, brightly, across the street and left Jerry standing alone at the fountain. He was the happiest man in New York.

VI

Ordinarily, the subway ride from Central Park to Greenwich Village was insufferably boring for Jerry. But this night it was exquisite. Sitting sideways on the seat in the uncrowded train car and pulling his knees up to his chest, he rested his head against the cool window. He spent the ride looking at his reflection and thinking of Jenny.

Mrs. Calamesa's television was still going strong when Jerry let himself into the building. The dog continued to scratch and the cats went on with their moaning. But the old lady didn't care. Her number-two heartthrob had just come back to late night viewing. She sat beneath her comforter, a cup of warm milk at her side, and clung to every dimpled smile of Dick Cavett.

After closing the door behind him, Jerry scooted up the dark hallway, rounded the landing and dashed up the last flight to his attic flat. It wasn't until after he had finally fumbled his keys into the lock and opened his door that he noticed the note taped beneath the hinge.

Tossing the keys onto a small table by the door and switching on the overhead light, he yanked the note down and read it out loud to himself: "I saw you looking at that girl. You're full of shit, too. Love, Helene."

Jerry smiled wryly and sniffed as he shook his head. Then he pulled off his tie and kicked the door closed.

Just as he was about to latch the double security locks, the phone rang. He whirled around, startled by a call at that late hour.

Instinctively moving toward the telephone, he reached down to lift the receiver at the third shrill ring. Then he stopped, his hand suspended in midair. Instead of answering the insistent phone, he dropped Helene's note next to it, flicked off the light and crossed to his bedroom.

The phone rang two more times and then fell quiet, its chiming echo lingering in the living room for a few more seconds.

VII

Sunday, after meeting in mid-afternoon, Jerry and Jenny spent most of the day wandering through the upper floors of the Museum of Modern Art. The day before, Jerry had purchased a large toy for Benjamin and he carried it in a Macy's bag held loosely under his arm. An exhibit of American watercolors had just opened the previous week and Jerry insisted that they pass a good deal of their time viewing his favorite style of painting. Jenny was easy to please. She participated in lively, knowledgeable discussions with Jerry about some of the more impressionistic works. Then she stood by respectfully as Jerry found himself transfixed by a painting that depicted a storyteller and a bevy of eager children seated at his feet. After a few minutes he turned away and she took his arm to lead him upstairs to the black and white photography display.

The day passed peacefully for them. They were together and doing exactly what they wanted to do. As the sunlight faded in the twilight, they crossed the lobby and entered the sculpture garden. Once they had ascended the few steps to the raised platform on the right, they huddled in the chill fall air and looked at the huge David Smith stainless steel sculpture. Others about them offered their approvals and interpretations in hushed tones, and after a while, Jerry squeezed Jenny's waist and asked, "Do you like that?"

"All the times I've been here, I've never been able to decide." She raised her eyebrows and winked. "I always spend my time wondering if it likes me."

"Really? I've had my problems with it, too." Jerry said as they walked around to look at the far side of the massive reflecting piece. "I've even gone so far as to say it's an overdeveloped object of sculpture."

They stopped and he noticed a young woman tilting her head in his direction, trying to listen in. "I don't mean I ran around the garden yelling it out like a nut," he continued. Then he leaned toward the woman and winked. "It was sort of a nasty whisper, rather than a fullblown yell, you know?"

The other woman smiled weakly, tugged at her knit cap and walked away. Jenny elbowed Jerry in the ribs and tried to scold him for being so rude, but they both fell into a fit of the giggles as they watched the same lady sidle up to another couple and lean in to eavesdrop on their conversation.

Jerry threw his arm casually over her shoulder and toyed with the tassels of her royal blue knit scarf. "Jenny?" he began, "where's your husband today?"

"He's probably still at his office."

"On a Sunday?"

"Well, it beats being with your family." She reached up and folded her fingers into his. "Anyway, he's taking a client out to dinner. He said he'd be late."

Pulling his hand away, Jerry took Benjamin's toy and held the bag in front of him with both hands. "You haven't told me anything about your marriage."

"I will," she sighed. "I'm having too good a time now." Then she pecked him on the nose, looped her arm through his and started for the stairs. "Come on. Let's go see what the movie is."

The poster on the easel by the door announced a Charlie Chaplin festival. They only had to look at each other for an instant and they knew they had something else in common. Jerry paid the usher, and taking Jenny's hand, stepped into the darkened theater.

The room was pitch-black and crowded. Charlie Chaplin balanced on a teetering ladder precariously perched on a flag pole high up on a tall building. In the corner, an organist tried gamely to punctuate the action with stirring chords of lightfingered patter.

Holding the bag in one hand and Jenny's hand in the other, Jerry bumped and tripped his way to a pair of seats near the center of the third row. Once seated, Jenny immediately became engrossed in the movie. She withdrew her hand from Jerry's and placed both hands on her knees as she sat forward and laughed vigorously at the antics on the screen. Jerry just shifted around and watched her, content with the thought that she was finally relaxing and allowing herself to have fun at last.

The tempo of the organ music changed abruptly and the scene showed Chaplin chasing after a young boy up and down a hallway full of doors. The kid would go in one door and Chaplin would follow. But then the boy would come out another door at the other end of the hall. And so on. It had been done a million times, but never this simply, never this well. Finally, the Little Tramp just waited in the hall with his arms crossed, tapping his foot. Sure enough, the kid came storming out of one of the doors and ran smack into Chaplin's arms. The comedian swooped him up and waddled down the hall. The crowd loved it.

Jerry tapped Jenny on the back and, when she turned to him, he whispered, "Hey, I almost forgot." He handed her the large Macy's bag. "This is for Benjamin. That kid up there just reminded me."

"What is it?" she whispered, placing the package on her lap.

"Open it and see."

Excited at the adventure, Jenny gripped the bag in both hands and tore at the paper. Under the best of

63

circumstances, this would have made considerable noise. But the sound of rustling and tearing paper was augmented tenfold in the quiet theater. A chorus of angry shushes were blown their way until she managed to get all the paper off the toy.

Once it was free of its wrapping, she held it up to the light of the screen to be able to see it better. The shadow of a large wooden caterpillar with wheels and a sectioned body crossed the screen.

Someone in back yelled out, "For Christ's sake, lady!"

Jenny hurriedly pulled the toy down with a loud tinkling of the bells attached to the long, bouncy antennae. The shushes came again until everyone around them was out of breath.

Jenny held the brightly painted caterpillar on her lap and looked at Jerry. "It's beautiful," she said, delighted with the gift. "He'll adore it!" She leaned over to kiss him on the cheek and one of the antennae twanged out of her hand and set its bell to chiming.

A thick-shouldered fat woman in the seat directly in front of them turned around to direct a killer's stare at Jerry.

"See if you can sort of muffle the bells, would you, Jen?" Jerry pleaded.

But once he said that, the shushers took up another moist, airy chorus and Jerry was annoyed with their impatience. "Relax!" he shouted. "It's a silent movie!"

This, of course, only served to incite the crowd even further. But when Jerry reached over to retrieve the caterpillar, he accidently bumped the antennae and they tinkled away madly for almost a minute as he and Jenny fumbled to quiet them. The movie-loving patrons were on the verge of becoming a mob. The beefy woman in front spun around in her seat and pointed a stubby and menacing finger at Jerry. "Some of us are trying to enjoy the film!" she announced in a hoarse whisper.

"You could be deaf and enjoy it!" Jerry retorted. "No offense, *sir!*"

At this, Jenny became convulsed with laughter and the caterpillar jiggled clamorously on her legs. Not only were the bells jingling, but the wooden body sections were now clacking together and creating quite a racket. The audience failed to see the humor of the situation.

Discretion seeming the better part of getting out of the theater alive, Jerry grabbed up the toy and said, "I think it's time to take this thing for a little walk." He took her hand. "Come on."

Together, they stepped on toes and bumped into knees as they stumbled their way to the aisle. Then, while the others watched angrily, they made their way up to the lobby doors. Just as they were about to go through, Jerry whispered, "Wait," and they stopped. Holding the toy by its tail section, Jerry shook it for all it was worth; and the bells no longer tinkled, they clanged. The wooden sections no longer merely clacked, they crashed. The people shushed themselves senseless as Jerry and Jenny, laughing and holding their sides, made their escape.

VIII

After sharing a dish of butter pecan ice cream at Rumpelmayer's, Jerry and Jenny casually strolled the evening away along Central Park South. Tipping imaginary hats to the doormen of the finer hotels and impetuously asking cabbies for directions to places that didn't exist, the two of them goofed and traipsied their way toward her apartment. A couple of kids on a puppy-love romp.

Passing by a row of modest four-story buildings, Jerry was in the middle of animatedly retelling a story about his first sexual non-encounter at the age of twenty. Just when he was about to imitate the part where the police flashed their lights into the back of his parents' station wagon, Jenny grabbed him by the collar and directed him toward the entrance of her apartment complex. When he stopped to take in the sheer enormity of the place, not to mention the grandiose detail, his postadolescent escapades were soon forgotten. Standing in the middle of the sidewalk and tilting his head back as far as he could, Jerry could barely see the rooftop tennis courts thirty-five stories above.

He mouthed a silent, reverent "Wow!" and turned toward Jenny. But she had already entered the courtyard and was headed for the main doorway. Jerry scooted after her and came up behind her just as the doorman held open the door.

"Good evening, Mrs. Moore," the tall black man

said. He was dressed in a dark green uniform with brilliant gold braiding and a smart black cap. George Jessel would have loved it.

Jenny smiled pleasantly. "Good evening Martin," she said as she went in.

The doorman was about to let the door swing closed when Jerry stepped forward. Pushing his hat back on his head, he scrutinized Jerry from head to toe and back again before sticking out his foot to stop the door from closing all the way.

Sensing that this was as good as it was going to get, Jerry said, "Hiya, Martin," and hustled through the slim opening. The caterpillar in his arms bobbed and weaved with every step.

Jenny held the elevator door open for him. Once they were both inside, she pushed the button for the twenty-second floor and leaned back against the gold-flecked wallpaper. Jerry sat on the leather bench with the toy in his lap, and looked at his reflection in the mirrored ceiling. The thought crossed his mind that the elevator was furnished better than his rich uncle's home in Long Island.

"Are you sure this whole thing is okay?" he asked Jenny, looking at the top of her head in the mirror above them.

"Yes," Jenny answered, smiling indulgently. "Preston never gets home before one when he's out with a client."

The elevator came to a smooth stop and the doors slid apart neatly. With Jenny in the lead, they walked down the long, poshly decorated corridor. Dripping chandeliers and stately portraits of Victorian generals lined the hallway on both sides.

"Well, suppose ol' Preston just happens to walk in," Jerry said ogling the opulent but suffocating decor. "Who am I supposed to be? The caterpillar delivery man?"

"A world-famous, unpublished author," she laughed

as she stopped at the door to her home. "Jerry," she began, touching his cheek gently, "I really don't care if he walks in. Okay?"

He pressed his face into her hand. "Okay yourself."

Jenny drew her keys from her purse and opened the door to her apartment. But it only opened a few inches until it was stopped by the security chain.

"Flora?" she called. "It's me."

"Just a minute," someone responded from inside.

They heard footsteps on the tile from within and then the door was pushed shut. After a few seconds of chain rattling and knob turning, the door was opened again and Flora stood aside for Jenny and Jerry to enter. The housekeeper, a plain middle-aged woman with gloomy grey hair and the world's worst taste in clothes, was already dressed in her pastel green rain slicker and white, ankle-high cowboy boots with red tassels. A feathered derby and a soft-pink, flowered fabric handbag with her name ironed on in yellow gingham letters completed the outfit. She was agitated about something and watched Jerry even more suspiciously than Martin had as he followed Jenny inside.

"Did Benjamin wake up?" Jenny asked as she unbuttoned her coat.

"No," Flora answered, still staring warily at Jerry. "But I think he's getting a cold. He's sort of snuffling in there."

"I'll go look at him. Thank you, Flora." Jenny handed her housekeeper a five-dollar bill. "Ask Martin to get you a taxi. Good night. I'll see you in the morning." And with that, she took the caterpillar from Jerry and hurried down the hallway toward the bedrooms to check on her son.

"It's after ten o'clock," Flora yelled after her. When Jenny didn't respond, she turned to take it out on Jerry. "She said ten o'clock at the absolute latest," she implored, pointing an accusing finger at him as he retreated.

"Uh, I, uh, didn't know—" Jerry began his defense.

"Forget it!" she snapped. She pulled up her collar and stepped into the hallway. "Good night," she said without looking back.

"Good—" Jerry started to respond, but Flora closed the door between them. "—night."

Left alone and to his own devices in the strange home of a new friend, Jerry immediately went about what came most naturally in such situations. He snooped around. First, he took in the quiet splendor of the simple but elegant foyer. White tiled floor, straight-backed cane chair, bevelled and framed mirror over a dark marble shelf.

Stepping down two steps onto the lush persimmon carpet of the living room, Jerry inspected the many fine photographs and Folon prints over the deep-brown sectional couch. A broad glass-and-chrome coffee table separated the couch from two matching easy chairs, each beneath its own chrome-globed reading lamp. A richly textured oriental rug served as an appropriate wall-hanging on the far side of the room next to the white brick fireplace. Bamboo-slat curtains were parted slightly to reveal a terrace with a spectacular view of Central Park.

Passing through a short hallway toward the kitchen, Jerry stopped to look at a handsome print of Picasso's *Man with the Blue Guitar*. Something about it disturbed him as it hung in perfect symmetry alongside several smaller pictures. That was it; everything was too perfect, too ordered. He glanced down the main hallway to see if Jenny was about, and satisfied that he was safe, he tilted the framed Picasso to an awkward angle. This, of course, made the entire wall look out of kilter. Immensely pleased with himself, Jerry stepped into the dining room.

A huge, antiqued, gold-and-white table was surrounded by eight chairs upholstered in contrasting velvet. A similarly appointed hutch in the wall to the left towered over the scene, and a swinging door between two dainty teacarts led to the kitchen.

The kitchen was fashioned in keeping with the rest of the apartment. *Gourmet* magazine-exquisite, it featured a thick butcher block in the middle of the blue-tiled floor over which hung a wide, wrought iron ring from which dangled every imaginable copper and pewter pot and utensil. A microwave oven was on the counter between an Osterizer and a Cuisinart machine. And next to the double oven and stove stood a tall, dark blue refrigerator. In the corner between the service entrance and the hallway door, a ponderously large, matching blue upright freezer claimed dominion over the rest of the room.

"The baby's fine," Jenny announced as she came into the kitchen. Jerry slammed the door closed. Caught in the act. "Flora's not happy unless she thinks he's getting a cold." She smiled at Jerry and winked. "I put the caterpillar in the crib with him."

"You know," Jerry began guiltily, "this place doesn't fit you at all."

"I know," she sighed as she hooked her thumbs in his belt loops and kissed him on the chin. "Basically, in my heart, I'm threadbare. But it's Preston's idea of how the successful executive is meant to live." She swept her hand around the room. "He takes guests on tours. I can't stand it." Pushing him backwards into the freezer door, she needled him. "I see you've discovered our latest elephantine attraction."

"Well, I couldn't help but—"

"That was just delivered this morning," she interrupted him teasingly. "As soon as he fills it, it's part of the grand tour."

Jerry allowed her to press closer and, just as he was about to devastate her with a ravishing, patented, Jerry Green lip-tingling kiss, there came the sound of a window breaking in an apartment on an upper floor. Glass clattered against the side of the building and shattered on the cobblestones of the courtyard far below. Not one to lose his cool at every little disturbance, Jerry jumped six inches off the ground and bumped foreheads with Jenny on the way down.

Other than the injury to her forehead, Jenny was undisturbed by the sound of the breaking glass. "Pay no attention," she advised, as she rubbed the spot Jerry had just struck. "A lot of windows have popped out recently. They keep telling us that the building is settling. Comes with the rent, I guess."

"Oh. That's reassuring."

Jenny took his hand and guided him through the short hallway into the living room. When they passed the crooked Picasso, Jerry said, "Tell me about Preston."

"Why?" she asked as they crossed to the two easy chairs.

"I'd like to know," he answered simply and sat down. As soon as he took his seat, the pressure of his body activated the overhead reading lamp.

Jenny pushed aside some oversized picture books and sat in front of Jerry. "Just put the whole thing into words? I don't think I can. Love, and then—not love." She put the toes of her tennis shoes onto his loafers and stared at her feet.

"I thought he was the golden boy. I had absolutely no doubts. And I was so wrong." She picked at a thread on the cuff of her jeans. "I think everybody used to look at us and say 'wow' all the time. And then one day, for no reason I can explain, I knew it wasn't so." She paused, working it out in her mind before going on.

"He's not what I thought he was. There is no golden boy. We only *looked* good together. No more than that." Her voice wavered, but there was no doubt that she was strong enough to continue. "Or maybe *I'm* not what I thought I was. I don't know anymore." Jenny looked up to Jerry, with tears that would not fall glistening in her eyes. "But there's nothing left. We're just going through the motions—and it's nobody's fault."

Jerry reached over and stroked her hair. She took his hand and kissed it on the palm and then held it between both of hers.

"Maybe the whole idea of marriage is too fragile," he said.

"No. It's not the idea that's fragile," she countered. "It's the people who aren't strong enough to survive each other." She let out a wry laugh. "How's that for wisdom?

"I don't know. But I have three things to tell you that pertain to this," Jerry said. "One, I'm an instantly breakable person—"

Jenny played with his fingers, clasping and unclasping hers in his. "I don't believe that," she said. "You're not, and neither am I."

Jerry rose from the easy chair and the light went out, allowing a warm, subliminal moonglow to be cast throughout the room. He sat on the picture books next to Jenny and put his arm around her waist. "Wait," he said. "Number two—I'd marry you in four seconds. Fragile or no fragile."

She turned to look at him, a smile quivering in the corners of her mouth.

"And three, I love you so much I don't even understand it." He looked away, embarrassed.

Jenny leaned over and took his face in her hands, forcing him to look directly at her. She held him for a few seconds before saying, "I love you too, Jerry."

"You do?" Jerry asked incredulously. This was all so unbelievable to him that he almost laughed out loud. He just couldn't cope with those words coming from this magnificent woman, directed at him. Not possible. He sat there, his face in her hands, for more than a minute.

"I can't believe it. Why me?"

"Why you, indeed?" Jenny asked him. "Why me?"

72

This was too much for him. Jenny had to know that she was absolutely everything any man could ever want, he thought. More than everything. He could only shake his head in shocked, joyous wonder. "Why you?" he repeated.

Lifting her arms onto his shoulders and folding her fingers behind his neck, Jenny was about to respond with a kiss when the sound of Benjamin's laughter came to them from his bedroom. A healthy, hearty, baby's laugh drifted down the hall and warmed them both.

"It must be the caterpillar," Jenny said, and she rose and headed for his room.

Jerry caught up with her just as she opened the door to the baby's room, and they both looked in. The room was bathed in soft yellow hues from a Woody Woodpecker night light. Rubber Disney characters dangled from a crazy mobile above Benjamin's crib. The baby boy lay on his side and giggled as he twanged the tinkling antennae on his new toy.

Jenny held her finger to her lips, pulled the door closed, and motioned for Jerry to tiptoe with her to the end of the hall. They stopped in front of the last door and listened. The laughter had stopped.

"At his age," Jerry whispered, "if I woke up laughing in the middle of the night, the enema would've been connected in thirty seconds."

Holding her hand over her mouth to keep from laughing, Jenny shook her head and begged Jerry with her eyes not to make her crack up. Then she took his arm and led him into the master bedroom.

A small bedside lamp threw gentle shadows across the room. The bed was obviously of Preston's choosing, as big as an aircraft carrier. Identical dressing tables bookended a vast his-and-hers bureau, and a large, overstuffed chair sat in the corner off the master bathroom. On the other wall, by the windows, was a small, cluttered desk. Jenny's desk.

Jerry crossed over to the desk and flicked on the brass piano lamp. A large sketchpad was propped against a dictionary. A series of watercolor caterpillars and flowers dappled the pages and, as Jerry flipped through the book, he came upon a thin, cheery caterpillar with 'Benjamin' written beneath it.

"This is beautiful," he said in hushed admiration as he turned to her. "They all are."

"I love you," Jenny said and hugged him close.

They kissed for a long, lovely, giving moment. When Jerry came up for air, he rubbed his nose against Jenny's and said, "It's so overwhelming, I don't even know what comes next. I can offer you instant poverty and an employees' discount at Macy's."

"That's more than I deserve," Jenny said. "I accept."

Letting her go, Jerry went to sit on the low window sill. "Wait a minute. Did I just ask you to marry me, and did you say yes?"

"Uh-huh."

"And Benjamin goes along with the deal?"

She nodded in affirmation and smiled.

"And you're sure?" Jerry had to ask. He still couldn't believe it.

Jenny came to him at the window and put her arms on his shoulders. Then she kissed his hair and said softly, "Yes. I'm sure."

Taking her wrists as he stood up, Jerry continued to shake his head in disbelief. "This is unreal. Two minutes ago we were talking about the breakability of marriage, and—"

But Jenny bit him on the ear lobe to shut him up and whispered, "I love you. We'll be the judges of how breakable that is, okay?"

This time when they kissed, there was less urgency and more trust. Each of them prolonged the embrace and helped to make the sweet caress linger. They kissed casually, confidently, each freely giving and accepting.

Jerry happened to open his eyes for a second and spotted a middleaged couple on the terrace across the courtyard watching them. He broke off the kiss and turned Jenny around to see.

"Look," he said. "Spectators."

Jenny shrugged, not caring the least about this uninvited audience. "Think we should take bows?"

"Nah. Why don't we just wave with casual abandon?"

And they did. Standing side by side and smiling proudly, they raised their right arms and, in unison, waved with what they imagined to be casual abandon.

The couple abruptly backed off the terrace and through their sliding glass doors. The drapes then were pulled shut and their light was turned off.

"Well," Jerry laughed, enjoying the victory. "That makes six."

"Six what?"

"People who know about us. Not counting strangers. Unless you want to count them—" He pointed out the window to the recently vacated balcony across the way. "—as stranger."

"No, let's consider them acquaintances," she said. "After all, we waved."

"Okay. There's your rich friend who called you Jenjamin. God, that's really horrible. *Jenjamin.*" He grimaced and stuck out his tongue to register his displeasure at the nickname. "Then there's Helene, the girl I was with, and the doorman, your maid, and the voyeurs over there. That's six. Count 'em folks."

But Jenny couldn't care less who knew. "Right. Now if they each tell two friends," she teased, "and they each tell two more—"

She was interrupted by the sound of the front door opening. "Jen? You home?" came Preston's voice from the foyer.

Jerry almost shrieked with fright and Jenny hurried to close the bedroom door.

"Preston" she said, in an uneasy whisper.

"That makes seven," Jerry said and then kicked himself for not being able to keep his sense of humor in control.

They huddled together by the door and listened to the sounds coming from the front part of the apartment. First there were footsteps, then another door opening, followed by a muffled conversation between two men.

"He's got somebody with him," Jenny whispered, her eyes wide with excitement. "There's a service entrance. I could go into the living room and distract them while you—"

Jerry kissed her hard on the mouth to stop her from talking. He shook his head 'no,' and held her head so that she had to look him in the eyes.

"Jenny, do you love me?" She nodded. "Good," he said. "And do you really want to divorce him and marry me?"

She nodded again.

"Then we might as well tell him now," he said with as much bravado as he could muster. "We'll just wait until the other guy leaves."

"I can tell him after you slip out," Jenny tried to persuade him. "I've thought about it so many times, and I've never—" She hugged him. "Now I know I can do it."

Lowering himself on one knee, Jerry cocked his ear at the doorway and tried to listen to what was going on down the hall. "Hey, we're together," he whispered. "Why should you have to do it alone?"

They heard footsteps crossing the tile of the foyer and padding through the dining room Then the conversation grew louder, but no more distinguishable, as the two men walked across another set of different-sounding tile. Their laughter drifted back to the bedroom.

"They're in the kitchen now," Jenny said.

There followed the sound of ice being cracked out of an ice tray and the cubes falling noisily into an ice bucket. Then came a markedly different noise, a blunt thudding sound. Indefinable, yet somehow distinct. Hurried footsteps across the tile, soft padding, then more tile.

"What was that noise?" Jenny asked as she tugged at Jerry's collar and urged him to rise from his knee and hold her. He wrapped his arms around her and shrugged.

They heard the front door open and close. And then nothing. Silence. Pulling open the bedroom door, they stood together and waited.

Absolute, unmoving silence.

Jerry drew a huge breath. "Okay, he's alone. Are you ready to tell him?"

Jenny nodded and they started for the hallway. But Jerry hesitated and pulled her to him. They kissed. "For good luck," he said, before going on.

Hand in hand, with Jenny slightly in the lead, they walked down the hallway. The weight of what they were about to say to Preston really hadn't dawned on them yet. To sneak around together in the bedroom while the man of the house entertained a guest, and then to break the sort of news they were going to hit him with—the mere notion of it all was so overpowering that they couldn't begin to cope with it. They were operating on nervous energy, firm resolve, and love. And that was all they needed. When they came to Benjamin's bedroom, Jenny stopped briefly and squeezed Jerry's hand before taking the last few steps to the kitchen doorway.

"This is going to be awkward as hell, but we'll manage." Jerry smiled weakly as they turned into the kitchen together.

The lights in the kitchen were all burning brightly and Jenny, a little ahead of Jerry, was the first to see it. She gasped in horror and buried her face in Jerry's

77

chest. Then he saw it, too, and his knees turned to liquid. He was afraid he was going to fall over in a faint. He let out a little scream and the two of them clung to each other, trembling and terrified.

IX

Preston Moore, athletic and ruddy businessman, man of good taste and impeccable fashion, the paradigm of the executive on the rise—Preston Moore lay slumped face down across the butcher block. The dark brown handle of a nine-inch kitchen knife protruded from his back just to the left of the center seam of his Yves St. Laurent sport coat. Wrapped around the knife handle was a pale yellow dish towel, already beginning to stain with the color of seeping blood. A mahogany ice bucket was on its side under the butcher block and ice cubes were strewn everywhere, melting into tiny pools that trickled into the cracks between the blue tiles.

Consumed by paralyzing terror, Jerry clutched Jenny tightly to his side. They held onto each other for support, for strength. Although it was a dreadful sight, both were transfixed by the macabre scene, almost hypnotized, and neither could turn away. They just stared in shocked silence.

But then Preston's body, through some invisible force of gravity, started to slide off the butcher block. Alarmed, but still frozen in place, Jerry and Jenny watched in numbed horror as the corpse slid to the edge, teetered for a second, then fell heavily to the floor with an indelicate *thunk*.

This was too much for Jenny and she screamed at the top of her lungs. Her high, frightened scream spurred

Jerry into action. He grabbed her and spun her around so that she was no longer forced to look upon her husband's body. But in so doing, he was still facing the grotesque form on the floor.

"Oh, my God," Jenny sobbed into his arms as a violent shudder coursed its way through her body.

Jerry stroked her hair and held her close until she calmed. Then he pulled away and, making sure that she wouldn't be able to see, he moved closer to Preston's body.

He inched his way across the floor until he was next to Preston. Swallowing hard against the nausea welling inside, he forced himself to kneel down next to the still form at his feet. The knife, undisturbed by the fall, remained in place. But the dish towel had fallen away, making painfully evident the steady flow of blood that matted the jacket around the wound and was just beginning to work its way down to the floor.

Doing what he knew must be done, but not without trepidation, Jerry reached out and felt for Preston's pulse. He let his hand stay around the wrist for a long time, hoping against hope for a glimmer of life.

There was none.

Reaching up to the counter for support, Jerry pulled himself upright and crossed his arms in front of his chest. He stared at the body on the floor, the blood forming a thick pool at its side. Then he turned to check on Jenny. She still had her back to the scene, her arm resting on the doorjamb and her forehead resting against her arm.

The enormity of the predicament slowly dawned on Jerry. He stood there with his back against the tiled counter and worked his jaw, clenching and unclenching his teeth, causing the tiny muscle in his temple to bounce rhythmically. The man of the house is found stabbed to death, he thought, by his wife and another man after they have just been witnessed carressing in the bedroom. It didn't look too promising. And it was obvious that they were in a lot of trouble. Circumstantial evidence could send them away for a lifetime.

"First things first," he said to himself in a low whisper. He crossed the kitchen and put his arms around Jenny. She shuddered at his touch and he closed his arms securely around her. Kissing the back of her head as he led her from the kitchen and into the hallway, he leaned in close and whispered softly, "He's dead, Jenny." Then he turned off the harsh lights and ushered her toward the living room.

"Oh, my God . . . Oh my God . . . ." Jenny repeated through her sobs as she allowed herself to be led into the living room. At first, Jerry was going to seat her in one of the easy chairs, but this was no time for the automatic reading lamp to come on. It was as if such illumination would invade their precious solitude. So he guided Jenny to the couch and helped her to sit in the corner of the largest section. As soon as she was seated, she grabbed up a throw pillow and clutched it to her lap like a child holding a stuffed toy for comfort.

"Stay here," Jerry said, as he kissed her on the forehead. "I'm just going to look outside. Okay?"

Jenny picked at the pillow and nodded silently.

Moving quickly, Jerry stepped up into the foyer and unlocked the front door. Then he cautiously poked his head out the door and looked to his right. The elevator light indicated that it was stopped at the ninth floor. After peering to his left and making certain that the corridor was empty, Jerry came back into the apartment and locked, bolted, and chained the door.

When he returned to the living room, Jenny was resting her head on the arm of the couch. The pillow was still in her lap and her eyes were red from crying.

Jerry stood on the other side of the glass coffee table and pondered the alternatives. One thing was certain: Preston was dead and he and Jenny would look like prime suspects unless they could figure something out. But fast.

"Jenny, I want you to do something," he said after a minute. "I mean right now." She lifted her head from the couch and waited for him to continue. "Is there a house phone down to the doorman?" he asked.

"Yeah," she said in a small voice.

"Where is it?"

Feebly, she tilted her head toward the front door and said, "In the foyer."

"Come with me," Jerry said, and took both her hands in his to help her up off the couch. She was still dazed by what had happened and yielded to Jerry's assistance helplessly.

Once he had her standing, Jerry paused a moment to let her get her bearings. Although still a little wobbly, she seemed to be much steadier than she had been earlier. After a minute, Jerry put his arm around her waist and took her to the foyer steps, indulgently taking his time as they went.

Jenny clung to the brass railing as she climbed the two steps and pointed to the white wall phone next to the mirror. "We should call the police," she said.

"Not till you speak to the doorman," Jerry replied. He had a plan and was determined to see it through. "Just say, 'Is the gentleman who come in with Mr. Moore still down there looking for a taxi?'" he instructed. "I'll tell you what to say next."

But Jenny was feeling woozy again. She reached out to the marble shelf and slowly sat on the high-backed chair.

"Can you do it?" Jerry asked urgently. "It's vitally important."

She nodded, and Jerry lifted the receiver off the wall and held it to his ear. Then he pushed the button to call the doorman and knelt down next to Jenny. Still holding the receiver to his ear, he twisted the phone around so Jenny could speak into the mouthpiece while he listened.

A moment later, Martin came on and said, "May I help you?"

Jerry pointed to Jenny and she began to speak mechanically, as if her voice were not a part of her being.

Without emotion she asked, "Martin, is that gentleman who came in with Mr. Moore still down there looking for a taxi?"

As Martin replied, Jerry's face registered his disappointment. He put his hand over the mouthpiece and told Jenny what to say. "Sorry," he coached. "He's playing some kind of joke on me. Thanks very much."

Then he removed his hand from the phone and Jenny repeated in that same, unfeeling voice, "Sorry. He's playing some kind of joke on me. Thanks very much."

With a frustrated sigh, Jerry reached up and replaced the receiver on the wall. Then he helped Jenny rise and held her close, trying to borrow some strength from her. But she stood there in a trance, unable to give.

Realizing that he must continue to control the situation until Jenny came around, he said, "Your husband came in alone."

Jenny looked at him questioningly, not understanding the implication. But the implication of the combined circumstances was driving Jerry crazy. And it was beginning to show as it wore him down.

"Come on," he said urgently, the muscle in his temple doing its number again. "Let's talk this through and figure out what to do." He stepped down into the living room and turned to offer his hand to Jenny. But she suddenly came to her senses, brought back to reality by Jerry's agitation. Jenny realized her responsiblity in the predicament and braced herself to face up to it.

"What do you want me to do?" she asked, as she joined Jerry in the center of the room.

Pleased to have her back, he squeezed her hand and said, "Let's talk it through and see what happens. We'll think of something."

Jenny sat on the coffee table and watched Jerry pace between the two easy chairs. "I don't understand about talking to the doorman," she said. "Why don't we just call the police?"

Jerry stopped for a second and placed both his hands squarely on the back of the far easy chair. "Jenny," he said firmly, "we can't call the police."

She was uneasy about the prospect of not having the police involved immediately. She felt compelled to do what was right, to get the police there right away and explained what happened to Preston. "Why not?" she asked.

"Because," Jerry began, looking her squarely in the eyes. "It's going to look to them as though we killed him."

Jenny raised her hand to her open mouth as if to stifle a gasp.

"As though *we* killed him? she repeated, horrified and confused. "How can they think that?"

Pacing again at full throttle, Jerry explained. "Everything points to it, that's why. Did he have a lot of life insurance?"

"Yes, but God, Jerry—the police can't possibly—"

"Look." Jerry interrupted as he reconstructed the evening for her as well as for himself. "You and I came up together, and I didn't leave, and then your husband came up alone."

He moved over to the terrace window and closed the bamboo curtains. "Nothing's been stolen. I mean it's not a robbery or anything, and—" He turned back to face her and held out his arms. "—What am I doing here to begin with? They've got to ask that."

Crossing to the bar, he thought of fixing the two of them a drink. But then he remembered where the ice bucket was and he decided he could do without a drink after all. "Well, sir," he went on as if speaking to an investigator, "we were in the bedroom during a casual visit I made. Just a little kissing; nothing more, I assure you."

Jenny followed his every nervous motion. It was as if, should she turn away, she would be alone. Desperately, she pursued him with her eyes, refusing to let him go.

He came around to the front of the chair and stood over her. "And those people who saw us kissing in there?" Jerry held up an imaginary newspaper and read the headlines. "Husband surprises lovers. Lovers stab husband with kitchen knife." He dropped his hands. "That knife is from your kitchen, isn't it?"

"Yeah."

Jerry blew out a long breath, and in his anguish, slapped at the lamp hanging over the easy chair. The globe swayed back and forth at crazy angles like a boxing bag. "He couldn't have brought his own knife, could he?"

He reached up to steady the bouncing lamp and said seriously, "Jenny, we've been seen falling in love by at least six people! And your marriage was on the rocks to begin with. Somebody else must know that."

Sitting on the picture books next to Jenny, he draped his arm over her shoulder and dropped his head disconsolately. "And the life insurance? Even if we tell the police the absolute God's-honest-truth, they won't believe a word of it."

He was up again, walking in small circles between the chairs. Jenny watched as he spoke. "Jenny," he asked, "is there any reason you know of that anyone would want to kill your husband?"

Groping behind her across the table, she grabbed up the throw pillow and held it tightly to her breast. "No," she said, shaking her head. "Why?"

"Because we—you and I—have what appears to be a reason, a motive," Jerry said loudly, furious at the circumstances. "That's why. Does that explain it?"

For the first time that evening, the full impact of what had been troubling Jerry finally hit home. Jenny choked on her words and the tears began to come anew. "Oh, God, I don't know what—"

"I was afraid you'd agree. For sure, the police will." Jerry's mind was racing way ahead of his ability to reason. His pacing brought him to the foyer steps and he sat on the top one with his elbows on his knees and his chin cupped in his hands.

When Jenny shifted around to look at him, he went on. "Look, we could break up the place and throw all your jewelry down the incinerator or something imaginative like that, and try to make it appear like a robbery." He wrote that idea off even before he finished saying it. "And we could tie each other up, but why would a burglar kill him and not us?"

"And we've already called the doorman," Jenny offered.

"To ask about the gentleman who came in with Mr. Moore." Jerry pulled at his hair in frustration. "I know. I know."

"Why did we do that?" Jenny asked.

"Because if somebody had come in with him," Jerry said as he rose, "—and why should we have thought otherwise?—Then we could call the police." He caught his reflection in the mirror. Not liking what he saw, he turned away and stepped down into the living room. "It was a chance," he said in despair. "We took a chance and lost. The doorman'll remember that call."

As he came toward the couch, he saw that Jenny's head was bent forward and the tears were streaming down her face. They collected at the tip of her nose and, one by one, fell to the pillow in her lap. She was crying silently.

Jerry knelt before her and took her face in his hands. Then he gently kissed away the tears and blew softly on her eyes. "How do you feel?" he asked.

Rubbing her cheek into his palm, she answered, "I don't even know. I—" Jenny took his hands and held them in her lap. "Jerry, a long time ago, I loved Preston. And I can remember times that were so good."

She started to cry again. When she tried to turn away, Jerry put his hand on the back of her neck and urged her to talk to him.

"Just the incredible thrill of deciding to get married," she went on haltingly, "—and that first year—I know it all went away and finally I didn't like him at all. Not at all." She grabbed his wrist and laid her head down on his forearm. "But he was my husband, and he's dead, damn it! And Jerry—" She leaned in until their foreheads were touching. "I can't believe it happened. I feel so sorry for him."

Jerry kissed the tears from her nose and whispered, "I know, baby. I know."

"They're going to suspect us, aren't they?" Jenny asked.

"I think they'll arrest us, Jen," Jerry said soberly.

A trembling passed through her body. Whatever slim reserve she had mustered, abandoned her. She closed her eyes and whispered to herself, "Benjamin—"

Jerry stood up and stroked her hair. "I know. I wasn't going to mention him yet."

She looked up and started to rise. But the weight of the trauma defeated her. "Oh, God, Jerry," she sobbed. "We have to think of something. We can't just—" Her eyes pleaded for an answer. "What'll happen to Benjamin?"

"This may sound totally insane, but there's no other way I can think of." Much to his own surprise, Jerry could feel a plan coming on. He had always prided himself on being able to get out of whatever jams he'd stumbled into. But this wasn't just another jam; it was life and death and the first woman he'd ever loved.

Speaking slowly, he shared his thoughts. "We have to do it ourselves," he said. "We have to find the murderer—" Jenny started to interrupt, but he wasn't finished. "*And* we have to force him to confess."

87

"How are we going to do that?" Jenny asked, her shoulders and her spirits sagging simultaneously. She had been buoyed by Jerry's momentary enthusiasm, but as soon as she heard what he had in mind, her hopes plummeted.

"I haven't the faintest idea," he admitted. "We also have to hide the body—uh, Preston—somehwere, without being seen."

"But—"

"Listen. We know what we have to do, we just don't know how," he reasoned, before she could protest. Then he continued, "It's either that or call the police right now. And I don't think they'll believe us."

He decided that he'd interrupted her enough times for one evening. After all, it was her house, her marriage, her baby and her dead husband. It was time to let her talk. He waited.

After a minute or so of uncomfortable silence, he prodded her. "Jenny?"

She looked up to him, her blue eyes red-rimmed and wet. "It's a horrible decision to make," she said, and then, in a voice that almost sounded like a moan, she said, "Okay. Where do we begin?" and turned away.

The pressure was on and it was time to do some heavy plotting. Jerry did what he always did in this situation. He paced, his jaw flexing, the muscle in his temple keeping perfect time.

"We begin by thinking," he announced, trying to formulate a plan. "Whoever killed your husband has to be somebody he knew. We heard them talking. Right? Right."

Jenny went back to being a spectator as he paced. Clutching the pillow tightly to herself, she raised one foot onto the coffee table and rested her chin on her knee.

"They came into the apartment together, but the doorman didn't see them enter the building together." Jerry went on piecing the puzzle into place. "How the guy managed that, God only knows. But he did." He hastened his steps as his thoughts came more rapidly. "Okay. *Why* did he kill him? That's the big question."

After posing the question to the room at large, he settled into the easy chair to ponder the answer. "Wait!" he exclaimed, holding up his finger. An idea had struck home, at the same instant the reading light above the chair came on. The irony escaped Jerry, and Jenny was too amazed at the coincidence to comment.

"Whoever the killer is," Jerry explained as he worked through his idea, "he expects a big headline in tomorrow morning's papers." He underlined each word in mid-air with his finger as if the paper were suspended before him "*Insurance Executive Murdered*—or whatever."

Putting one foot up on the coffee table and leaning forward, he outlined his new plan to Jenny. "But what does he do if there's nothing in the papers at all—no mention of it—because we didn't call the police?"

Jenny wasn't about to respond, but Jerry excitedly held up his hand as if to keep her from answering. It was his baby now. "He goes *crazy*, that's what he does! He has to find out what happened. And where does he find that out?"

Another rhetorical question that Jenny knew better than to try to answer. "Here!" Jerry exclaimed as he jumped to his feet, his eyes sparkling. "Here, that's where. And then we'll have him."

Jerry stopped to catch his breath, and Jenny knew that if she had any questions, she'd better interject them at that moment. "Suppose he just decides to wait it out and see what happens?"

"Exactly!" Jerry shouted. He clapped his hands together excitedly. Then the logic of what Jenny had just said hit him between the eyes and the wind left his sails. "Oh," he said. "We'd definitely have to consider that—possibility." He sat on the arm of the chair.

Jenny threw the pillow back on the couch and

reached over to touch Jerry's arm. "Well, what would the police do? I mean, if they were us?" She seemed to be coming out of her funk. Although far from cheery, she was no longer debilitated by her grief. Realizing the urgency of the moment and the necessity for her to be as helpful as possible, she adjusted to the spirit of what they both knew had to be done.

Grateful for her change of demeanor, Jerry patted her hand and replied, "I guess they'd question everybody he ever knew. We can't do that."

He stood up and gazed toward the kitchen as if he'd be able to divine some information from the scene of the crime. "The police would find out who he had dinner with tonight," he pondered. Then a thought occured to him and he was suddenly alert.

"Jenny," he said as he pulled her up to stand beside him. "Who *did* he have dinner with?"

Jenny simply shook her head. "I don't know," she said regretfully.

But Jerry had a notion and he was determined to see it through. It was the first slender thread of direction they'd had since they discovered Preston's body. "Did he carry a memorandum thing with him? A date book?"

"Yeah. In his wallet."

A mixed blessing. They definitely needed to know what Warren had written in his date book. But the prospect of going back into the kitchen and actually removing it from his person was not too appealing.

Jerry looked at Jenny and immediately knew that he was elected. Process of elimination. There was no way she was about to do it. "Okay," he said gamely as he started to fidget. "So I'd better get it. From his pocket. In the kitchen there. That's what I'll do. Okay." He inched forward. "Right in the kitchen there. That would be a—positive approach. Something constructive." Just about out of things to mumble, he broke away from Jenny. "So that's what I'll do. Here goes."

Jenny sat back down on the coffee table and watched

apprehensively as he headed for the kitchen. Now that she was alone, the trauma of the evening overpowered her once again and she laid back on the table and stared at the patterns on the ceiling. A single tear streamed down the side of her face and meandered toward her ear. She didn't bother to wipe it away.

Without turning on the light, Jerry stepped into the kitchen and strode to the body. But his false bravado abandoned him as soon as he saw Warren spread out on the floor just as he'd left him. Bathed in the moonlight flowing in through the window over the sink, the grotesque sight burned itself into Jerry's memory forever.

Squatting down next to him, Jerry reached out and touched Preston's shoulder. The mere contact of his finger sent shivers up his spine and he pulled his hand away as quickly as if he'd grabbed a hot stove burner. After doing this two more times, Jerry swallowed hard and held onto Preston's shoulder. He was committed.

As soon as his hand grew accustomed to the touch, he heaved forcefully and was just able to turn the lifeless form onto its side. The head lolled awkwardly and Jerry did everything he could to keep from glancing at the agonized face frozen in a startled question at the instant of death. Working quickly, more out of terror than efficiency, Jerry searched the pockets of Preston's pants and coat. As he pulled items out, he tossed them onto the butcher block until he was satisfied there was nothing else to find.

He let the body loose from his grasp and it plopped back to its original, face-down position, the knife quivering with the impact. Then he rose and inspected the contents of Preston's pockets that were spread out on the block. A ring of keys, some change, a comb, a cuticle knife. That was it. No memorandum book. No wallet.

"Nothing," Jerry muttered, shaking his head in frustration.

It became increasingly apparent to him that if, indeed, he and Jenny were going to attempt an investigation on their own, now that no date book was to be found to make their task simpler, something would have to be done with the victim's body. They couldn't very well leave it where it was, face-down and oozing in its own elaborate kitchen. And getting it out of the apartment presented more problems than Jerry was prepared to tackle that particular night.

Just as he was about to scoop up the stuff from Preston's pockets, the motor of the huge upright freezer whirred to life. It was so obvious that it probably wouldn't work, Jerry thought to himself as he went to the freezer and pulled open the door. One lonely carton of Schrafft's ice cream and what seemed like acres of empty, available space.

Quickly, he tossed the ice cream into the sink and measured the width of the freezer with his hands. Then, with his hands still spread apart, he crossed back to Warren and compared the width of his shoulders to the opening. It would definitely be tight, but it just might work. Stooping low and bending at the knees, Jerry put his hands under Preston's arms and lifted.

Actually it was closer to dragging than lifting, but he managed to get the late Mr. Moore over to the cavernous appliance.

X

A short while later, Jerry and Jenny sat together on the couch looking through the things from Preston's pockets that were piled on the coffee table. The tense energy that had substained them over the previous few hours had been displaced by a profound weariness and both of them showed signs of the tremendous strain.

"Where else could we have put him?" Jerry asked, as he urged Jenny to lay back and put her feet up. "I mean, there was no way we could have gotten him out of the house. And even if we did, then what?"

She didn't respond. She couldn't. She just continued to stare vacantly at the ceiling, her only movement an occasional blinking away of a tear. Jerry put his hand to her cheek. "Jenny," he said softly.

Slowly, she turned her head and faced him. The devastation of her loss and her predicament were etched clearly on her harrowed face. "It's just—well, the whole thing is so—so irreversible now," she said.

Jerry nodded in solemn affirmation. It was evident that he would have to provide the strength for both of them for the time being. "Agreed. So there's only one thing we can do, and that's to move ahead. Now, what we have here," he indicated the keys, comb, and other things heaped before them, "is a promising step backward."

Looping his little finger through the metal key ring,

he lifted the keys and held them out to Jenny. "What are these for?"

"The usual," she said as she draped her arm across her forehead. "The house. The car. I guess some of them are office keys."

Straightening up alertly, Jerry dropped the keys back on the table and announced, "I forgot about the office! They'll be expecting him there tomorrow morning." His shoulders drooped. "God, how do we handle that?"

They both knew it was time for him to pace again. Jenny pulled her legs aside to allow him to pass from behind the coffee table to where he'd have more room to roam.

Jenny was exhausted. The comtemplation of any more conspiracy defeated her and she cried out, "Jerry—I'm so tired now that I just can't—I have to sleep for a little while." She folded her arms across her chest and looked to him, her eyes pleading.

Without hesitation, Jerry stepped back around the table and sat on the floor by her head. Reaching for the Afghan blanket that was draped across the arm of the couch, he covered her legs and settled down next to her, stroking her hair and cheek.

"I'm sorry," she said meekly.

"Ssh. You just sleep," Jerry comforted her.

She smiled and turned to look at him. "Stay with me," she said, and then closed her eyes.

Jerry leaned forward and kissed her lightly on the lips. "I'll be here."

He reached under her and put his arms around her. Hugging her close to him, he rested his head next to hers on the throw pillow and within a few minutes they were both asleep.

XI

Although they didn't sleep very well that night, Jerry and Jenny were up early the next morning. In the fog of half-sleep, Jerry stumbled to the bathroom and doused his face with cold water. This woke him up enough to bring back the miseries of the evening before and the responsibilities of the day ahead. Grabbing a towel to dry his face, he came back down the hallway to see what Jenny was up to.

She'd been busy in the few minutes Jerry was in the bathroom. The drapes were opened on a cool but cozy morning and Benjamin sat in his baby-seat happily munching on saltines. Jenny came into the living room with a bottle of milk for the baby and set it on the tray of his walker. She sat on the arm of one of the chairs and bent down to pick up the caterpillar Benjamin had just toppled to the carpet.

The baby reached eagerly for the toy and accidently sent the bottle tumbling to the floor. For some private toddler reason, this delighted him and he squealed with laughter. Just as Jenny was about to replace the bottle, he whacked the caterpillar and sent it flying. But Jenny was in no mood this particular morning for carousing with her son. She flushed with anger and was about to scold him when the baby held out a soggy cracker and offered it to his mother.

Jenny's temper melted. She picked up the bottle and the toy. Then she accepted the saltine in exchange for a healthy hug for Benjamin. After watching this scene from the hallway, Jerry came in and draped his towel over Jenny's shoulder. When she stood up, he kissed her once on the nose and took her hand.

"Come on," he said as he led her toward the telephone on the end table. "Let's get this over with."

Seating Jenny on the couch and himself on the edge of the end table, he coached her on the call she was about to make. "The doctor just left. Preston's got the flu. Plus laryngitis," he said slowly as Jenny listened uneasily. "He can't talk at all, and he needs complete rest. You'll be in touch with them tomorrow." Jenny's eyes had drifted over to Benjamin and Jerry grabbed her wrist. "Can you do it?"

She continued to stare at her son, but she nodded as she pulled hand away. Jerry looked at his watch.

"It's nine-fifteen," he said. "Okay. Go."

As if struggling with some maternal magnetic force, Jenny slowly turned her attention away from Benjamin and picked up the receiver. She closed her eyes and whispered some private encouragement to herself before dialing the number to her husband's office.

It was still early at the executive offices of Magnum Insurance Underwriters. The mailroom boy was making his first rounds of the day and only a few typewriters in the vast secretarial pool were occupied. The few typists who, through circumstances beyond their collective control, had arrived before the nine-thirty starting bell, sipped at cups of steaming coffee, filed their nails or stared at the clock.

But Herbert Little was there.

Preston Moore's new secretary had been the first one on the floor every morning since his first day. He was that type of man. In his mid-forties and rather on the smallish side, his full mustache and painstakingly coordinated wardrobe elevated him to that obscure line between a stylishly efficient subordinate and a prissy fag. Whatever, he'd been getting the job done, and done well, since Preston had interviewed him and decided to brave a male assistant.

Herbert was just about to clean his wire-rimmed glasses and dive into the morning filing when the phone rang. His desk in the reception area of Preston's office suite was characteristically neat and proper, and the girls in the typing pool had been having a field day watching him and his obsessive mannerisms. Taking a paper clip from the magnetic holder, he marked his place in the filing and straightened his ruler so that it was parallel with the edge of his blotter. This done, he lifted the receiver on the third ring.

"Mr. Moore's office," he said cordially, a slight Brahmin tinge floating on the word 'office.'

Jenny had forgotten that Preston had hired a male as his secretary and she was startled to hear a masculine voice on the other end. "Mr. Moore's secretary, please," she said as she gripped the phone tightly. "This is Mrs. Moore."

"Oh, good morning, Mrs. Moore!" Herbert chirped. "This is Herbert Little. I'm Mr. Moore's new secretary." He arranged the envelopes according to size as the mailboy dropped them into his receiving basket. "I'm afraid Mr. Moore hasn't arrived yet. Can I give him a message?"

"Uh, well, no. Actually, he's here," Jenny said, looking to Jerry for encouragement. He nodded and urged her to continue. "I'm calling to let you know that he's ill. The doctor just left. It seems he has the flu."

Jerry waved his hand across her eyes to get Jenny's attention. When she looked up, he clutched his throat and opened his mouth.

"And laryngitis," she added quickly. "He can't talk at all. He really feels terrible."

The mailboy had stopped to eavesdrop and Herbert turned his swivel chair around after shooting him what would have to pass for a threatening look. "Oh, I'm very sorry to hear that, Mrs. Moore," Herbert consoled her, his voice reflecting his disappointment. "Is there anything we can do to help?"

By this time, Jerry had maneuvered himself closer to Jenny and she held the phone away from her ear so they both could listen. When Jenny looked to him for an answer, he gravely shook his head.

"That's very kind of you," she said, "But no. He just has to stay in bed and rest."

"He mustn't rush it. The flu can be nasty," Herbert advised. The mailboy was just about to stick his head through the open door to Preston's inner office and snoop around when Herbert spotted him. He snapped his fingers twice and tried to shoo the kid away. "Well, I'll notify everyone here, Mrs. Moore," he offered in a kindly voice as he shot daggers of contempt at the intrusive teenager. "And if there's anything I can do, please let me know."

"Thanks very much," Jenny said. "Goodbye."

"Goodbye, Mrs. Moore," Herbert said, and slammed the receiver down. "My second week here and he's got the flu!" he complained. "That's really helpful."

The mailboy listened to this tiny tantrum for a second, then scurried away to tell the girls in the other room.

Jenny still held the phone in both hands. She couldn't put it down and the tears came up to sting her eyes again. Jerry had heard Herbert ring off, but didn't want to be too forceful with Jenny during a difficult moment.

98

So he waited until he saw the tension pass from her mood. Then he took the receiver from her and hung up.

"That was perfect," he said brightly, trying to inject a little optimism into both their spirits.

Jenny stared at the phone. "Every single word sounded false," she said blankly. Then she mimicked her own conversation contemptuously. " 'It seems he has the flu—' "

But Jerry interrupted her with a kiss. She reached out for him and clutched him to her side, hanging on desperately.

"It sounded fine," Jerry said easily. "Jenny, that was just his secretary, not the district attorney."

Jenny stiffened as soon as he said this and he knew it was the wrong thing to say at precisely the wrong moment. He still had his infallible sense of timing.

"Disregard everything I said after 'secretary.' " Then he looked at his watch and started to rise. "I'm going to be late."

Still holding onto his hand, although he was standing and she remained seated, Jenny looked up and said, "I wish you didn't have to go to work today." Her eyes moistened.

Jerry grabbed both of her wrists and yanked her up playfully. "It'll look better if it at least starts out like a normal day. I'll be back at lunch time." His arm over her shoulder and her thumb hooked in his belt loop, they moved toward Benjamin. "I'll call you every half hour and I'll make some kind of excuse to get the afternoon off. Maybe I can develop a toothache or something."

Benjamin had knocked the caterpillar off his baby-tender and again was trying to play with the toy with his feet. He let out a squeal every time he jumped in the seat and the whole contraption bounced closer to the bells of the antennae. But just before he got to where he could reach the caterpillar, the commotion he was creating caused the bottle to topple off the tray and crack against the side of the coffee table. Tiny specks of glass and a thin trickle of milk worked their way into the carpet.

"Great move, Benjamin," Jerry said gaily. "Where do you keep the rented mop, Jen?"

"Don't bother," she replied with a nonchalant wave of her hand. "Flora can clean it up when she gets here."

Then it hit her. She froze in the middle of the living room, her hand still in midair. "Flora!" she shrieked. "Oh, my God. I forgot all about her!"

"Flora?" Jerry asked tentatively, not quite sure he believed that anything else could go wrong.

"The maid. She'll be here any minute," Jenny said, her eyes searching the room as if she were looking for some place to hide in her own home. "That ice cream we threw away was her breakfast."

"Just don't let her in. That's all." It seemed simple enough to Jerry. "Tell her she's got the rest of the week off. They have ice cream all over the city. She can eat somewhere else."

Figuring that he'd just talked the excitable Jenny down from another potential panic, Jerry stopped to pick up the bottle and clean up the mess. But, just at that moment, they heard a key in the front door and then the sound of the door being stopped by the security chain.

Still in his crouched position, he jumped three feet in the air and came down running. "I'll sneak out the service entrance!" he called out in a loud whisper as he fled.

Hesitating only an instant in front of the freezer, Jerry scrambled through the kitchen and bolted out the back door. Some internal signal sent the freezer's motor whirring to life and it stood humming smoothly in the kitchen —first a witness and then an accomplice in this bizarre chain of events.

After she heard the back door close, Jenny stepped

up into the foyer and released the chain. But she held her ground in the doorway and firmly refused Flora access to the apartment.

"Good morning Mrs—" the maid began to say as she tried to pass. She was wearing an imitation leopard-skin coat over a paisley double knit pantsuit. A clear plastic shopping bag dangled over one arm.

"Flora—" Jenny said quickly, as she steadied herself in the doorway. "This was really a fantastic last minute decision, but we're all going on a little trip—uh, actually it's a big trip, and so you have the rest of the week off, or more, with pay." The maid stood there, a surprised and skeptical expression on her face. "I know how surprised you must be—"

But Flora had things on her mind, and if nothing else, she prided herself on being efficient and loyal. "I've got a lot of cleaning to do," she protested as she leaned into the door.

Jenny inched the door closed. "We'll just let the dirt accumulate," she said, kicking herself for not coming up with something better. Jerry would have handled this cleverly, she thought.

Flora eyed her cynically. "But you know how I hate that." Then she added quickly, as if to catch Jenny off guard, "Where are you going?"

"Uh, France," Jenny answered after only a slight pause. She was getting better at this. "The south of, uh, Cap D' Antibe. That's in France." Pressing her body into the same space that Flora occupied, she began to edge the maid back out into the corridor. "So you just have a wonderful rest and I'll call you when we get back."

Flora was almost completely out of the apartment, but she still retained a small bit of territory at the threshold. Jenny was actually straining against her maid's immoveable body as she said, "Remember, with pay. Full pay. We just decided to go this morning, so I didn't have a chance to—"

But Flora broke into Jenny's ramblings. She no longer cared for the Moores' problems. It was time to think of herself. "What am I supposed to do all week?"

"Whatever you want," Jenny said as she finally squeezed the rest of her housekeeper and her shopping bag into the corridor. "What an opportuity to go to the movies! On full pay." She started to close the door. "Look, I have to pack. We're leaving any minute. Enjoy yourself!" And she slammed the door, double-locked it and replaced the chain. Then she fell back against the door and wrapped her arms around her body. She was trembling as she whispered "Oh, God," to herself and went to take care of Benjamin.

Out in the hall, Fora stared at the door for a while, a strange quizzical grin beginning at the corners of her mouth. She raised herself up on the toes of her cowboy boots and tried to peak through the peephole. But all she could see was the reflection of the inside of the door in the foyer mirror. The grin worked itself into a whimsical smile as she turned for the elevators.

At that same moment, Jerry was barrelling down the twenty-two flights in the back stairwell. The floors blurred by as he careened around landings and recklessly tore down the steps.

On the tenth floor, a kid was hacking away at the lock of a bicycle that was chained to the railing. He glanced up when he heard someone flying down like gangbusters toward him. But before he could split, Jerry was past him, huffing and puffing his way to the ground floor. The kid looked over the bannister briefly and went back to work on the bike.

Jerry hit the street and broke into a jog. But the cold morning air slapped him full in the face and he came to his senses. Slowing to a passably respectable trot, he weaved his way through the rather heavy pedestrian traffic and made his way to Macy's.

He was late for a change.

XII

Because it was a full half-hour after opening time, Jerry was able to walk into Macy's through the main entrance. His mind was in a thousand places at once and none of them had anything to do with work. He half wished that his supervisor would approach him. If he was going to have to take any lip from anyone this morning, he knew it would be his last day of employment at the store. He didn't care.

The sale had ended the previous weekend so there was only the moderately heavy morning shopping contingent to contend with as Jerry worked his way back to the time clock. When he passed through the swinging doors to the employee's lounge, his supervisor was at the water fountain filling a styrofoam cup. Jerry tensed, but pressed on. He pulled his card from the slot and was about to insert it into the machine when he noticed something unusual. The card was already punched. Someone had punched him in on time. A few minutes early, in fact.

Glancing around furtively, he replaced the card and whisked past his supervisor. After crossing the main floor, he took the escalator up the two flights to *Bambini* and made his way toward his counter.

That was when he noticed Helene. She was at his display stacking Macy's shopping bags in their cubicle beneath the counter. As soon as Jerry saw the contrite expression on her face when she saw him, he realized that it was she who had covered for him this morning.

Perhaps things were getting better between them, he thought. Maybe she understood. "Good morning," he said sweetly. "Thanks for saving my life."

As soon as Helene opened her mouth, Jerry knew that he had been hoping for the impossible. "Look Jerry," she began as if she'd been rehearsing all weekend. "It was an infantile temper tantrum the other night. I'm the first to admit it."

Jerry's shoulders sagged as it became painfully clear that nothing had changed.

"And the entire weekend," she pressed on without skipping a breath, "I was punishing you by letting you ignore me. That's even more infantile." Helene came around from behind the counter and put her hand on his shoulder. "You know, justifying the unjustifiable—"

"Helene, for God's sake!" Jerry interrupted as he ducked away from her digging fingernails. There was no way he could deal with her this day. "I lost the whole train of thought on the first 'infantile.' "

Helene did her best to look hurt. "Listen to me," Jerry pleaded. "I've got customers all over the floor to contend with, and—"

"You've got another girl," she cut in as she toyed with the cameo necklace that rested on the shelf of her bosom like a mountain climber taking a breather on a ledge. "*That's* your problem. And she's married."

Her stinging tirade was laced with undeniable truths and Jerry was very uncomfortable. He passed by her and started stamping the day's date on his purchase forms. Anything to keep busy.

"That's your problem." Helene wasn't about to give it up. "But don't expect me to flounce off biting my lip. We're both free agents in the love game. And if you want to be a masochist, too, that's your business."

Jerry pounded the dating stamp so hard that the handle cracked. He looked to Helene, ready to join the battle and fight to the finish. But she was floucing off toward her own department. Angry and hurt, she was biting her lip to keep from strangling him.

"Excuse me, sir!" A young man stood at the costume rack and was obviously very annoyed.

Not having seen the man come around behind him, Jerry was startled when he heard the unpleasant voice. "By all means," he said cooly. "You're excused."

He tossed the dating stamp into the trash bin and hurried toward the down escalator. The customer stood at the rack, confused and indignant.

Helene watched Jerry's head dip from view as he descended on the moving stairway. Then, seething with pent-up fury, she went to take it out on the poor soul Jerry had just abandoned.

Downstairs, Jerry signed out and headed for Jenny's. It had been a hell of a morning.

XIII

The day doorman at Jenny's complex didn't think twice when the man wearing the Macy's delivery cap and carrying a large cardboard box strode through the delivery door. In fact, Wayland, the day man, held the door open for Jerry.

Once on the twenty-second floor, Jerry went around to the service entrance just to play it safe. He knocked and listened to the footsteps scooting across the kitchen floor. Then came Jenny's tentative voice. "Jerry?"

"Yeah. It's me."

The door opened and Jenny pulled Jerry to her. She was wearing a Notre Dame football jersey and brown corduroy pants. The morning had been difficult for her and she was relieved to have him back again. It was he who was providing the strength and direction during her catastrophe and she'd missed him dearly.

Jerry kicked the door closed and said, "No one even looked twice at me downstairs. How I'm going to get out again is another matter, but I'll worry about that later."

With Jenny shadowing his every move, Jerry crossed to the kitchen counter and laid the carton down next to the microwave oven. "In that box is Harvey Chortles, the talking teddy bear," he announced brightly as he took off his cap. "Benjamin'll go out of his mind with joy and—"

106

Jenny smothered the rest of his sentence with a kiss. "Oh, God," she gasped, "I'm so glad you're here."

Understanding that a little tenderness was worth more than some false levity, Jerry put his arms around her and drew her close. She trembled and put her head against his chest as he tried to soothe her.

"Hey, come on," he said softly. "We've got a lot to do. Are you all set?"

She let out a long sigh and pulled away enough to kiss him again. When she finished, she nodded bravely and took his hand. But she wasn't ready. Gently guiding her, Jerry looped his arm around her waist and led her into the living room.

"Where's Benjamin?" he asked when it dawned on him that it was far too quiet for a household with a toddler.

"In his crib," Jenny answered. "I don't think he's going to nap." She was nervous and it was obvious that the slightest provocation would shatter the delicate shield she'd erected around herself.

"Don't worry about him," he said as he took her coat from the arm of the couch and helped her put it on. "I'm a sensational pattycake player. It goes 'Richman, Poorman, Mailman, Doorman,' right?"

A smile crinkled along her lips and Jenny let out a little laugh as they stepped up to the foyer.

"Don't forget," Jerry reminded her, "You want his briefcase and his diary. And any notes you see on his desk—and I love you and somehow we're going to get out of this. I promise."

They clung to each other for a few seconds, neither wanting to open the front door. Each knew that they couldn't carry on like this everytime they came together or parted. Jerry pulled away, and trying to be casual, opened the door while Jenny busied herself with zipping up her coat and pulling on the hood.

Just as she was about to step into the hallway, the sound of Benjamin's delightful squealing laugh filled the apartment and they both smiled. Jerry winked reassuringly and, with a smack on her rump for good luck, sent Jenny on her way.

After he'd closed and chained the door, Jerry ran down the hall to Benjamin's room. As soon as he got there, he stopped to peek inside. The baby was standing in his crib, grasping the railing with both hands and rocking back and forth as he giggled at the motion of his bed.

Jerry smiled and longed for those ancient days when he had had as few worries as Benjamin. Shaking off the nostalgia, he came into the room and began a one-sided conversation with the kid as if he were talking with a contemporary.

"Why shouldn't we get out of this mess?" he asked. The baby stopped rocking as if to pay attention. "Once the clues start pouring in and the killer is forced to expose himself—" Benjamin didn't react to the possible implications of this double entendre, but Jerry felt obligated to smooth it over.

"That's only the pristine interpretation, kid," he explained. "We're free and clear, right?"

Benjamin was at a loss for words and could only mumble, "Eggeggeggegg," as he drooled on his shirt.

No longer wishing to entertain the baby or distract himself, Jerry sank into the overstuffed chair that was covered with toys and pillows. "Tell me a story," he implored dismally, "Anything with rabbits."

He grabbed his head with both hands, flopped back in the chair, and stared at the ceiling. Benjamin watched quietly, then began to chew on the caterpillar.

Downstairs, Wayland was just helping Jenny into a taxi when he said, "I haven't seen Mr. Moore this morning, Ma'am. He's usually out bright and early."

Jenny dropped her glove on the sidewalk and stooped

to retrieve it. "Oh. No, he has the flu." She stood up and climbed into the cab without meeting the doorman's eyes.

"A shame," Wayland sympathized. "That's miserable stuff, that flu. Tell him to take care of himself for me." He closed the door and stepped away.

"I will," Jenny said as the taxi pulled away from the curb. "Thank you, Wayland."

By the time Jenny's cab cleared the courtyard, Jerry had gathered himself out of his funk and was playing with Benjamin on the living room floor. Studiously applying himself to the construction of a Dixie cup pyramid, Jerry sat crosslegged in front of the fireplace. All this was supposedly for the benefit of the baby, who paid little attention to his babysitter and, instead, went to work sucking the fur off the ear of Harvey Chortles, the talking teddy bear.

Twisting the large stuffed animal around in his lap, Benjamin caught his toe in the plastic loop connected to the long string that activated its recorder. When he yanked it, the toy came to life.

"Hello there, youngster!" it chorused in a cheery, but tinny, voice. "My name is Harvey Chortles. What's yours?"

Benjamin clapped his hands gleefully and kissed the teddy bear on the nose. Then he went back to sucking on its ear.

But the energetic, happy voice of Harvey Chortles was grating on Jerry's frazzled nerves. "I hate you!" he hissed at the toy.

He dumped some more Dixie cups out of their box and returned to his construction—an indoor sandcastle for a big-city kid.

"Now concentrate on this, Benjamin, because I'm going to ask you some very key questions," Jerry said as if preparing a friend to listen to a long story. "Forget

109

how the killer got in without being seen. Let's get right to who did it and why. Okay?"

Having no objections so far, Benjamin took the plastic pull-string in his mouth and crawled off beneath the coffee table, with Harvey Chortles dragging along behind him.

"Key question number one," Jerry continued, disturbed by the apparent apathy of his audience. "Why does somebody who's not a burglar kill somebody else? He's fooling around with his wife? No, that's nonsense." The pyramid shuddered when Jerry affixed the next cup.

"The kill*ee* knows something which could incriminate the Kill*er*?" Jerry conjectured once the feeble structure settled. "That's a possibility." He chewed on this for a second. "Okay. What could he know?"

As he rose to stretch his cramped legs, an idea sparked. "Wait a minute!" Jerry got back on his knees and struck his head under the coffee table. "Tell me something, Benjamin. Did you ever notice that insurance companies play around with gigantic sums of money? Where do you think they get that money?"

If the baby knew, he wasn't talking.

"From selling policies that become automatically void if you try to make a claim. That's where," Jerry explained. "Go try to collect on your diaper rash insurance and you'll see what I mean."

Just then the doorbell rang and Jerry jumped up. That is, he would have jumped up if his head hadn't been under the coffee table at the time. After giving himself a pretty good lump on the back of the head, he extricated himself and successfully managed to jump up on the second try. Except this time be backed into the Dixie cup pyramid and it inelegantly collapsed into itself.

All this commotion excited Benjamin and he crabbed about the floor drooling and giggling.

Creeping stealthily toward the front door like a mem-

110

ber of the bomb squad on a dangerous mission, Jerry stood to one side and called out, "Who is it?"

"It's the police!" came the booming voice from the other side of the door.

XIV

It took a few seconds for Jerry to start breathing again. He stood slumped against the door, traumatized with fear. Finally, he pulled himself together enough to look through the peephole. Squinting one eye, he stole a look at the man in the hallway.

There are cops who look like everyone else and there are cops who look like the stereotypic, civilian's image of a cop. The man in the heavy trenchcoat, rumpled hat, and worn black shoes looked like he was born into a family of cops and had never had any doubts as to what his calling would be. He was tall, burly, and had the hammered face of a man who'd seen it all.

There were no alternatives for Jerry. Somehow, he would have to deal with one of New York's finest. Uncertainly, he reached for the doorknob and opened the door a crack. Bathed in the sliver of light from the corridor chandelier, the detective seemed more imposing that ever, larger than life.

"Could I see your identification?" Jerry asked uneasily. Then he quickly added "Please?" followed by a hasty, "Sir?"

Seemingly bored with it all, the cop pulled his hand from his coat pocket and neatly flipped open his wallet. A gold shield was pinned to one side of the leather and an N.Y.P.D. identification card was encased in the other.

Farrah Fawcett-Majors and Jeff Bridges co-star in . . .

Somebody Killed Her Husband

Jerry (Jeff Bridges) and Jenny (Farrah Fawcett-Majors)
meet over a box of spilled pretzels.

Jenny and husband Preston (Laurence Guittard)
having dinner at the Kitsch Inn.

Jerry and friend Helene (Patricia Elliott) dine across the room from Jenny and Preston Moore.

Jenny in a happy moment with her son Benjamin.

Phony detective Frank Danziger (Beeson Carroll) stands near the freezer where Preston Moore's body is hidden.

Jerry and Jenny realize they are being bugged.

Jerry and Jenny, in the apartment of Jenny's strange
neighbor, Ernest Van Santen (John Wood).

Jerry, incognito,
looks for some clues
in the death of
Preston Moore.

Jenny and Jerry forget their troubles long enough
to remember that they are in love.

Jenny in a
pensive moment.

Mr. Big—Herbert Little.

Jerry and Jenny
try to escape.

Herbert Little gives chase.

The lovers finally corner the man who killed Jenny's husband.

Jerry leaned forward to read the card. "Detective first-class Frank Danziger."

"That's correct," Danziger answered in a voice that echoed even when he spoke softly. He automatically flipped his wallet closed and said, "This is just a routine check."

After closing the door and releasing the chain, Jerry reopened the door and stepped aside. Danziger wiped his feet perfunctorily on an imaginary doormat and entered.

"You can't be too careful these days," Jerry explained as he led the policeman into the living room. "You could be letting in God knows what—whom. Uh, God knows whom. That's it." He laughed nervously, hoping for a bit of the same from the cop.

Nothing doing. This man was all business. Danziger unbuttoned his trenchcoat, tilted his hat back on his head, and pulled a neatly folded typewritten list from his inside coat pocket. His professional eye roamed the apartment, taking it all in with one practiced glance.

"You know," Jerry continued, trying to get through to this guy. "That's actually the first real police badge I've ever seen close up." He clapped his hands for emphasis. "Boy, it must weigh a ton!"

The cop ignored the small talk and unfolded the list. Then he took a ballpoint pen from his shirt pocket and looked at Jerry.

But Jerry wasn't done with his routine. "You could probably take some criminal and just hit him on the head with your wallet—" He fidgeted in place, his feet squirming in his shoes until the detective broke off his devastating stare and looked at this list.

"Apartment 22B," Danziger read from the sheet. "Moore. Is that right?"

"Right. What can I do for you?" Between the cop's cannonlike voice and penetrating stare, Jerry was a basket case. "How about three fingers of the smoothest im-

113

ported Scotch?" he offered as he allowed his feet to fidget their way toward the bar.

But as soon as Danziger spoke again, Jerry froze in place and awaited instructions. "Look sir," he said cooly, "I can be out of here in a couple of minutes if you'll just let me proceed."

"Oh. By all means," Jerry said, almost bowing to the presence of unchallenged authority. "Go ahead, Detective, uh—"

"Danziger. Are you Mr. Moore?"

"Me? No. No," Jerry chuckled, tossing his head from side to side. "Mr. Moore is out of town on business. I believe it's St. Louis this trip. And Mrs. Moore is out shopping." He paused while the detective made a few notes.

"I'm from Surrogate Mothers Limited," he offered holding out his hands in a demur shrug. "I'm just the babysitter." Jerry scoured the floor with his eyes until he spotted Benjamin under the coffee table. "That's the baby. Say hello to the nice detective, Benjamin."

"Look," Danziger cut in, his short fuse burning low. "Could I just explain why I'm here?" He almost paused to let Jerry respond, but thought better of it. "Last night a window was broken in the rear of the building. It's the third one this month." He took half a step forward as if to begin his investigation and Jerry retreated three steps until he was backed up against the easy chair.

"We think it's somebody with a BB gun or a slingshot," Danziger went on to explain as patiently as he could. "We're checking the apartments that have windows in the rear. So could I take a look in the back, please?" He noticed that Jerry's eyes were glazing over and he rapidly clicked his ballpoint pen twice with his thumb. Jerry rejoined the living.

He blinked and looked around as if just awakened from a dream. "In back?" he asked.

Danziger could no longer trifle with him. "That's

where the rear windows are," he said, without humor. He ground his teeth insistently and made it perfectly clear that he just wanted to do his job and get out of there.

"Yeah," Jerry agreed. "That makes sense."

He stooped down and dragged Benjamin out from under the coffee table. Then, with the baby in his arms, he motioned for the cop to follow as he headed for the hallway.

As they passed the paintings in the hall, Jerry turned to point out one of them to Danziger. "Picasso," he said proudly as if it were his own. When he turned to face forward again, he was in the kitchen—staring straight at the freezer.

"Kitchen . . ." he mumbled. He couldn't tear his eyes away from the freezer.

The detective nudged by him and went to the window over the sink. Leaning over the counter, he unlocked the window, opened it and looked outside. Whatever he did or didn't see evidently satisfied him and he pulled the window closed.

Then he came back to Jerry and asked, "You haven't seen a kid in the area with a BB gun or a slingshot, have you?"

"No, sir. Never in my life."

Danziger grunted something to himself and placed his checklist against the freezer door. As he jotted a few notes on the paper, using the appliance as a writing surface, there came a faintly audible "click" from the freezer. If the cop heard it, he didn't react. Jerry thought he heard it, but wasn't certain.

"Okay," the detective said as he turned back to Jerry. "How about the back bedrooms?"

"Surely," Jerry concurred, anxious to get out of the kitchen. He propped Benjamin up higher on his shoulder and led the cop down the hallway.

As soon as the three of them left the kitchen, the

freezer door slowly creaked open. At first it only parted a few inches. But then, as if it had a mischievious mind of its own, it swung wide open and thudded dully against the doorjamb. With the freezer door open all the way in this fashion, it would be impossible for anyone to reenter the kitchen without encountering the door and perhaps even observing the freezer's strange cargo.

Oblivious to what had just occurred, Jerry ushered Danziger down the long hallway and showed him into the master bedroom.

"This particular investigation must be a real mind-bender," Jerry said lightly as the cop inspected the rear window. "You know, all your years of technical police training finally coming to—"

Danziger slammed the window closed and sliced into Jerry with a treacherous stare.

"A little humor there . . . heh, heh." Jerry cowered behind Benjamin as the cop approached.

"The other windows have the same view?" Danziger asked, ingoring Jerry's ill-timed joke.

"Yes, indeed. Same thing."

The cop gestured for Jerry to lead him back down the hall. Shifting the baby to his other shoulder, he turned and started back toward the living room. But after he'd gone a few feet, he noticed the open freezer door filling the kitchen doorway.

Panic immediately got the better of him and he abruptly stopped walking, terror-stricken at the sight before him. Danziger wasn't paying attention and promptly plowed into Jerry from behind.

But Jerry was quick to apologize. "Sorry," he said as soon as he regained his balance. "That's definitely a no-fault situation."

Before the detective could respond, Jerry whirled around and raced for the kitchen. "Holy cow!" he shouted. "The whole freezer fell open!" He stopped in the doorway and whispered confidentially back to Danziger. "The 'holy cow' was on account of I can't say 'shit' in front of Benjamin."

As Jerry turned back to the kitchen he said, "I'll be right with you." The cop rested against the wall and watched him swing the freezer door shut.

Leaning against the door and pressing with all his weight to make sure it was secure, Jerry said, "They just don't make freezer latches like they used to, you know?" It seemed that Danziger didn't know, so Jerry left the kitchen and headed for the living room. "Onward," he said, bravely taking the lead once again.

As soon as Jerry walked onto the carpet, he stepped on a couple of Dixie cups, squishing them into flattened oblivion. When he knelt to put the baby on the floor, Danziger walked by and went to the bar to make some more notes. Turning his back to the cop for an instant, Jerry said to Benjamin, "Now we're going to have to find some more building material for our great pyramid, kid."

He ruffled Benjamin's hair and rose just as Danziger finished with his writing and folded his checklist. "Okay, that does it," the cop said, slipping the paper into his pocket. "Sorry to bother you."

"Oh, it's no bother at all." The detective nodded his thanks and made his way toward the foyer. At the same moment that Jerry arrived to show him out, Benjamin managed to get his toe caught in the loop of Harvey Chortles. He tugged with all his tiny might and the toy came to life.

"How'd you like to give me a nice, big, juicy kiss, cutey?"

Danziger closed his eyes and tried to pretend he hadn't heard what he knew he'd just heard.

"Uh, that's sort of a—" Jerry yanked the door open, "—a talking bear we have in there. Just a toy."

Without bothering to respond or look back, the detective stepped into the corridor. Immensely relieved,

117

Jerry closed the door softly and glanced through the peephole. Danziger's figure was receding down the hallway. The man looked tired.

Jerry chained the door and let out a tremendous sigh. Then he stepped down into the living room and went to the coffee table. "Benjamin," he started to say. Then he noticed that the baby wasn't in his customary hiding place.

"I love you, Mommy," came the boxed voice of Harvey Chortles, and Jerry turned to see Benjamin sitting under the bar.

"Hey, kid," he said, "How about a nap before we both get cranky?"

Squishing more Dixie cups along the way, he crossed the living room and bent down to pick up the baby. Taking Benjamin in his arms, Jerry started to rise, but his ascent was interrupted when he whacked the back of his head on the ledge of the bar. Struck dizzy for a moment, his knees buckled and he struggled to keep from dropping the baby.

Squatting down to the floor, he put Benjamin down and tenderly rubbed at the bump on his head. "Thanks. I needed that," he said, trying to find the lighter side to his headache.

When he looked up to inspect whatever damage his skull may have inflicted on the bar, something strange caught his eye. Raising himself to his knees, he brought his face closer to the underside of the bar ledge.

A small, black, metal box was fastened to the wood with some quick-drying adhesive. The white lettering written across it read:

ELECTRONIC SURVEILLANCE CORP.
TRANSMITTER—J8

Still rubbing the back of his head, but more from fear and confusion than pain, Jerry slowly sat back on the floor. It was as if he were melting downward into himself. He stayed very still for almost a minute, stunned and not quite prepared to believe what was happening.

Then he scooped up the baby and ran for the bedroom.

XV

The thunderous typing halted abruptly and the whispered gossiping just as quickly began, almost as if on some predetermined signal, when Jenny Moore strode through the offices of Magnum Insurance Underwriters. Such was the profound effect of her beauty, even when dressed in a football jersey and casual coat. The girls watched her pass and buzzed their jealous snipes to their neighbors. The office boys, their eyes wide and mouths dropped open, stood in spellbound silence. Only their heads moved slowly with her gliding passage.

Herbert Little had been notified that Jenny was coming. He straightened his tie and patted the wrinkles from his jacket as he waited for her. When she passed throught the doorway of the outer office, he virtually leaped to his feet and held out his hand.

"Mrs. Moore?" he asked. "Good morning. I'm Herbert Little."

Jenny accepted his hand graciously. "Very nice to meet you."

Herbert came around from behind his desk and closed the outer door in the mailboy's face. "I'm very sorry you went to all this trouble. We could have sent his things up by messenger."

"It's no trouble, really," Jenny protested. "Our pharmacy is in this area so I—we figured we'd kill two birds with one efficient stone."

"Well, then, it's a pleasure to finally meet you in person," Herbert said as he took her arm and ushered her into Preston's office.

"Thank you."

After they entered the office, Herbert released her arm and went to the mahogany closets on the other side of the room. Jenny, left alone briefly, quickly inspected Preston's olympic-sized desk for whatever she and Jerry might need. To her dismay, there were no papers of any sort in view. Only the usual desk ornaments: Tiffany silver ashtray, gold-faced clock set in clear plexiglass, matching onyx and ivory desk set, Gucci pencil cup, and the like. All very chic and overstated. All very Preston.

Something did catch her eye, though. Next to the telephone was a hand-tooled, leather-bound desk diary. Jenny stole a careful glance at Herbert Little's back and surreptitiously slipped the diary into her pocketbook.

"Here's his briefcase," Herbert announced at he shut the doors. If he had noticed Jenny's startled expression when he first spoke, he didn't let on. Joining her at the desk, he handed the elegantly thin attache case to Jenny and smiled.

"That's fine," Jenny said in a shaky voice. "Thank you."

Herbert nodded and pointed to the desktop. He may want his desk diary . . ."

"Oh," Jenny interjected a bit too suddenly. "I've already taken care of that, Mr. Little." She opened her purse to show him.

Herbert looked into the purse, then into her eyes, and finally at the recently vacated spot next to the telephone. "So you have," he said. "Good. He'll probably want to refer to it."

"Well, that should do it, then," Jenny said, and turned for the outer office.

Always the perfect gentleman, Herbert Little maneuvered his way around her and opened the door.

The mailboy still stood in the doorway. Not bright enough to think of an excuse for his presence, he just turned around and walked away. Jenny shook Herbert Little's hand and thanked him for his assistance before stepping out into the typing pool.

All work stopped until she reached the reception area and entered the elevator.

XVI

Every few minutes, Jerry would force himself to stop pacing so that he would check the living room carpet to inspect the trail he knew he was mashing into the pluch pile. Satisfied that the damage was probably only temporary, he resumed his agitated ambling. A sheet from Jenny's sketch pad was rolled into a tight cylinder in his hand and he used it to beat a nervous rhythm on his thigh as he walked.

As soon as he heard Jenny slide her key into the front door lock, he bolted for the foyer to intercept her.

The door opened a few inches against the chain and Jerry held up his hands to Jenny and said, "Just a minute, Mrs. Moore." After closing the door and releasing the chain, he let her in.

With the briefcase in one hand and her purse in the other, Jenny entered, mystified at the "Mrs. Moore" business. Before she could ask what was going on, Jerry crouched and held his fingers to his lips instruction her to be quiet and wait. Then he unrolled the sheet from her sketch pad and held it up for her to read: *WE'RE BEING BUGGED!*

Jenny gasped and started to say something, but Jerry put his hand over her mouth and guided her into the living room.

"Benjamin just fell asleep," he announced in a most efficient and subservient manner.

Laying her purse and the briefcase on the coffee table, Jenny felt compelled to say something. She questioned Jerry with her eyes, pleading for help.

He flipped the sheet of paper over and pointed to the other side which read: *I'M THE BABYSITTER*. Then he said a bit too loudly, "I think I wore the baby out. Heh, heh. Another ten minutes and he would've had me."

Motioning with his hands, he urged Jenny to play along, as if trying to persuade someone to join in a game of charades. She was terrified, but willing to go along with it.

"I'm—" she began, unsure of what to say. "I'm surprised you got him—to sleep at all." She screwed up her face and shook her head distastefully at her own bad acting. Then she held out her hands, palms up, as if to ask for approval.

Jerry nodded enthusiastically and gestured that they should both continue.

"So am I. I can state categorically, Mrs. Moore, that Benjamin is untouched by the energy crisis." He laughed out loud and signalled for her to do the same. "If you could only figure out a way to attach him to an engine—"

They shared another moment of empty laughter as Jerry led her to the bar and pointed to the listening device.

Jenny bent over and looked at the small black box. Then she turned to Jerry, frightened and unsure. But he instructed her to continue the stage whispers.

"I, uh, know what you mean," she said hollowly. "He's a regular dynamo."

By counting on his fingers and peeling bills off an imaginary roll of money, Jerry pantomined that she owed him a day's pay. It took some doing, but after a few more patient tries, she got the message.

"How much do I owe you?" she asked, speaking in

the direction of the bug like an amateur using a microphone for the first time.

Even as she spoke, Jerry was writing a new message on a clean corner of the sketch paper.

"Well, there's that four-hour minimum, Mrs. Moore," he began as he continued to write. "So that would be twelve dollars plus carfare. Thirteen-seventy."

He flattened the paper out on the top of the bar and waited for Jenny to read it. *SCULPTURE GARDEN— SAME BENCH—½ HOUR—DON'T TOUCH THE BUG.*

Swallowing against her fluttering stomach, Jenny nodded her understanding. Before she could say anything else, Jerry fled through the kitchen and out the service door.

By the time he huffed and puffed his way down to the tenth floor landing, he was too weary to notice that the bicycle was missing. A freshly severed piece of chain hung from the railing in mute testimony to the recent theft.

Pushing his tired legs beyond their normal endurance, he ran and stumbled down the remaining flights and headed for the museum.

XVII

There was the regular late-afternoon gathering of art lovers at the sculpture garden when Jerry arrived. When he first started down the familiar path, he noticed an older man sitting at his bench reading a newspaper. But just as he was preparing himself for his first panic in almost an hour, the man tucked the paper under his arm, rose and walked away. Scurrying past the couple in front of him, Jerry ran to the bench and stretched out.

About twenty minutes later, at precisely the moment Jerry had set aside for a nervous breakdown, he spotted her. Jenny was pushing Benjamin in his stroller along the path, trying valiantly, but unsuccessfully, to appear casual. Benjamin seemed quite as ease, though, as he calmly chewed on the ear of his Harvey Chortles toy.

Jerry stood up and took her hand as they both sat down together. He started talking as soon as they were reasonably settled.

"I don't like it. It's getting too confusing," he complained. "For the office and for your doorman, he has the flu. But for the detective he's in St. Louis on business because that's the first thing that popped into my head."

Jenny would have loved to soothe him, but she was just as wrought up as he was. She put one gloved hand on his knee and added, "And Flora thinks we're all away on vacation."

Slapping his head in disgust, Jerry moaned, "I forgot about that." He fiddled with her fingers and then intertwined his hand with hers. "Just keeping track of the lies is almost a career." He tucked one leg under the other and turned to her. "Here's another one: Whoever's listening to that bug thinks I'm a babysitter."

The frustration of the whole ponderous circumstance swelled inside Jenny and her eyes brimmed with tears. "But why did they put it there?" She almost whined. "They can't possibly know that Preston's dead, can they?"

To no one's surprise, and much to Benjamin's amusement, Jerry was up and pacing in tiny circles around the stroller.

"I don't know," he muttered. "I don't even know our next move." He stopped long enough to ask, "Are you sure there wasn't anything unusual in Preston's papers or his diary?"

"I couldn't find anything," Jenny shrugged as she followed his perpetual circumnavigation of the baby carriage. "I brought them for you to look at. They're in the canvas bag there on the stroller handle."

Halting in mid-step, Jerry reached into the carryall and pulled out the thin briefcase and the leather diary. He sat down again next to Jenny and held Preston's things on his lap. The briefcase promised to be the more difficult of the two, so he put it aside to deal with later. When he turned his attention to the desk diary, he noticed an unusal monogram on the cover.

"What's this?" he asked. "What does P.N.M.I.M. mean?"

"Oh. That's sort of a very expensive joke." Jenny waved her hand to dismiss its trivial significance. "The N.M.I. means 'no middle initial.' Preston doesn't—" She caught herself, realizing that she could no longer refer to her husband in the present tense. "—*didn't* have a middle name."

Jerry picked up on her discomfort at what she had just said and nodded soberly. "Preston N.M.I. Moore. Who gave it to him?" He chuckled. "I mean, a guy wouldn't buy that for himself. Not even Preston."

"No. It was a Christmas present from the Van Santens."

"Van Santen," Jerry repeated, mulling over the name. "The one who lives in your building. The one who saw us smooching at the fountain. That Van Santen?" As Jenny nodded, Benjamin, with his uncanny sense of timing, pulled Harvey Chortles' string with his mouth and the toy spewed forth another gem.

"Rub my tum-tum-tummy. It's all fuzzy-wuzzy," it requested in its singsong voice.

Chuckling out loud, Jerry rose from the bench to tussle with Benjamin. But he was startled when he heard someone behind him ask, "Whose tum-tum-tummy is all fuzzy-wuzzy?"

Spinning like a guilty top, he whirled to confront the intruder. As he turned, the briefcase and diary toppled to the ground. Fortunately for Jerry and Jenny, the diary fell with its monogrammed cover down.

Ernest Van Santen stood a few yards down the path with his wife Audrey. Ernest, dapper as always, was dressed in a dashing sharkskin coat complemented by a matching bowler hat and pewter-tipped walking stick. Audrey, perhaps sixty, fragilely pretty and not to be outdone by her younger husband, sported a full-length camel coat, high brown boots and an ermine cossack cap. Together, they presented the perfect picture of wealthy swingers on the constant prowl for eligible swingees.

Jerry exchanged an awkward glance with Jenny. As she rose to greet the approaching couple, Jerry stooped behind the stroller and just barely managed to get the briefcase and diary back into the carryall when Audrey came up to the baby.

"It must be Benjamin's tummy," she cooed in baby-talk as she tickled his moist chin.

"Well, it can't be Jenjamin's," Ernest decided as he kissed her hello.

Everyone except Ernest and the baby cringed at the silly name. "Oh," his wife admonished, "stop calling her that."

Jerry stood up behind the stroller and watched as Audrey bussed the air next to Jenny's cheek with a smacking high-society kiss.

"Sweetie! We haven't seen you in ages."

"Hello, Audrey. You look marvelous."

While Jenny responded in kind with an empty kiss of her own, Ernest knelt down and rumpled the baby's hair. "Now that is one hell of a bear, Benjamin," he said loud enough for everyone to hear. "May I?"

The baby didn't protest, so Ernest pulled Harvey Chortles' string and announced, "Listen to this, every-body!"

There was a pause followed by a winding, whirring noise. Then Harvey Chortles obliged his faithful audience. "I just love to be cuddled. Don't you?"

Feigning insult, Ernest slapped the bear lightly with a gloved hand. "That animal just made a pass at me."

He put the toy back in the stroller, and still laughing, turned to face the two women and Jerry. It was obviously time for formal introductions and Jenny rose to the occasion.

"This is Jerry Green," she said as evenly as she could. "Audrey and Ernest Van Santen."

"Hello," Audrey greeted him pleasantly.

"Hi, there," Jerry waved.

"How are you, young man?" Ernest said offering his hand.

"Oh, I'm, uh, swell thanks. Just swell," Jerry said as

they shook hands rather curtly. "How about yourself?"

But Ernest had already disengaged himself and was busy planting a series of wet kisses on Jenny's forehead.

"Now what's the meaning of all this?" he demanded between smacks. "Hanging out in the garden here with a perfect stranger."

"I was giving her tips on how to spot muggers," Jerry interjected. "The best way to tell is when their arm goes around your throat." He put his arm around his own throat as if this visual aid might help the joke. It didn't.

But Jenny saved the day. "Jerry's an old friend," she said gaily. "We grew up together."

Audrey clapped her hands, delighted at meeting someone new. But all the while, she scrutinized Jerry as if trying to fathom his intentions. "You don't mean you're from Buffalo, too?" she asked.

"Well," Jerry began, averting his eyes from her penetrating stare. "It's not the kind of thing a person readily—"

"Come on, Audrey," Jenny broke in forcefully, shooting Jerry a weighty look. "You know perfectly well I'm a born and bred Cincinnatian."

"Cincinnati*er*," Jerry corrected jovially. This old couple had put him off his stride just about enough for one afternoon. Now, thanks to Jenny's quick thinking, he was certain he'd be able to cope with them. "We've fought about that since we were kids," he said as he gave Jenny a friendly punch on the shoulder and shuffled his feet like a midwestern bumpkin.

The "old friends" routine was getting too mushy even for Ernest Van Santen. "Look," he said, breaking up the reunion. "We were just going back for a drink. Why don't you join us?"

"Oh, Well—" Jenny began to fidget, still rubbing her shoulder from Jerry's healthy lovetap. "I don't really think we—"

But Audrey would have none of it. "Of course, you will," she cut Jenny off. "You can leave a note for Preston to come over when he gets home from the office."

Jenny wished that she had been able to respond immediately, but she was at a loss for a moment. "Preston's in St. Louis—" she said awkwardly, "—on business."

"Then don't leave a note," Ernest decided, putting an end to her fumbling. "Come on, Mr. Green," he said to Jerry as he grabbed the handle of the stroller. "I'll wheel Benjamin and you can wheel Audrey."

"If you just give me a little push to get me started," Audrey began in the same teasing spirit. "I can make it on my own." She looped her arm through Jenny's and urged her down the path.

Ernest released the brake of the carriage and guided it with one hand. He casually draped the other over Jerry's shoulder and proceeded to follow the two women. Cringing only slightly, Jerry went along with the flow.

As they crossed the museum lobby, Jenny turned to exchange a mournful, helpless look with Jerry. There was nothing they could do.

XVIII

The Van Santen apartment, directly next door to Jenny's, was as indulgently decorated as their extravagant taste in clothes would indicate. They had plenty of money and they spent it vigorously on whatever they fancied. Consequently, their decor reflected a pastiche of fads spanning the previous ten years.

Plants were Audrey's private passion. Huge, leafy banana trees and rubber plants cluttered their own little acre in one corner of the living room. Interspersed among the larger greenery was an impressive collection of more conventionally sized plants, each with its own specially-timed, automatic growing light.

Modern sculptures and paintings echoing the various movements in art over the past decade filled all available spaces in the room. From towering anguished metal figures to tiny end table etchings with all the murals and centerpieces in between, the effect, ultimately, was successful. If nothing else, the Van Santens had somehow retained some semblance of taste and balance during their buying sprees.

A majestic white grand piano dominated the corner by the terrace window. Truly a beautiful instrument, its elegant presence was somewhat diminished by the papier-maché sculpted pianist seated at the keyboard. Hair flying, arched fingers forever poised and long coattails flowing, the stunning artifact assumed the appearance of a mad-genius composer. In the final analysis, the tenor of the piano and player was a cross between stately-sublime and campy-comical, not unlike the rest of the place.

The furniture was simple, but obviously chosen for its expensive and recognizable designer. A sun room had been constructed into one portion of the terrace and its three glass walls offered a breathtaking view of Manhatten at dusk. A chrome and glass bar was suspended from the rafters overhead and Ernest Van Santen set up shop in his favorite room. He was host and bartender and it was to be martinis all around.

"You just make yourselves at home. You always do," he called from the sun room as he mixed the cocktails in a crystal decanter. "Some really deadly martinis coming up any minute."

Audrey excused herself to go prepare a snack in the kitchen, leaving Jerry and Jenny alone with the baby in the living room.

"Why'd you agree to come here?" Jenny asked in a hushed voice as she watched Benjamin toddle about, pushing the stroller through the plants.

But Jerry was thoroughly engrossed in inspecting the elaborate setting he'd so unexpectedly found himself in. The watercolors above the couch were originals and quite impressive. And he still couldn't make up his mind about the piano. Jenny pinched him on the butt to get his attention, and he realized that she'd asked him a question.

"I agreed," he whispered, "so we wouldn't look sneaky." He turned full circle in the room. "God. Look at this stuff!"

"You kids want olives or twists?" Ernest called as he prepared to pour the vermouth into the tall flask.

"Yeah. Swell," Jerry called back as he searched for Benjamin in the foliage. He could hear him pushing the stroller around in there, but he couldn't see him.

"Twists," Jenny said as she approached the door to the bar area. "Not too strong, Ernest. I'm a mother."

"When I mix," Ernest winked conspiratorially, "think of yourself as a wench."

Just then Audrey turned on the stereo in the kitchen and rich symphonic music blasted at full force from the many speakers throughout the apartment. Such was the intensity of the music that the strings of the piano hummed and the glass rattled in the many picture frames.

"Christ Almighty!" Ernest muttered as, startled by the music, he inadvertently poured too much vermouth.

He set the bottle down on the swinging bar and shouted above the racket to Audrey in the kitchen. "Dear! Is that *Dawn and Siegfried's Rheinfahrt?*"

Jerry stood transfixed by the loud music, turning in his customery small circles as he tried to figure out the source of all the tumult. Cymbals crashed and tympani reverberated and Jerry had no idea what was going on. He would have put his hands over his ears, but he didn't want to insult anyone. He looked at Jenny. She stood calmly by the glass door, watching him, seemingly amused at his discomfort. Long accustomed to the eccentricities of the Van Santens, she placidly waited for round two of the stereophonic warfare.

"And what's wrong with *Siegfried's Rheinfahrt?*" Audrey shouted back as she came into the living room carrying an ornately decorated tray. Jerry ogled the feast in her hands: smoked oysters, onion dip, paté, water chestnuts, caviar, four types of crackers, and a glass of milk for Benjamin.

"*Rheinfahrt?*" he mouthed incredulously as Audrey passed by. Jenny stifled a laugh.

Not to be outdone, Ernest leaned over and pressed a button on his own massive stereo system. Different symphonic strains belted forth through the same sets of speakers and drowned out Audrey's selection. The piano strings jumped and the picture frames bounced against the walls.

"Brunhilde's Immolation Scene from Gotterdammerung!" Ernest screamed, as if issuing a challenge.

Jerry backed against the piano and gritted his teeth against the cacophony. Jenny serenely took a cracker from Audrey's tray and held it out near one of the banana plants. Benjamin's tiny hand flitted out, grabbed the treasure, and disappeared.

Suddenly the music stopped. The room still echoed with the residual effect of the potent sound system, like smoke after a battle, but soon the vibrations settled down and the last trace of the brief music war drifted away. The Van Santens had installed a failsafe device that would automatically shut down the stereo when the sound passed a certain decibel level. Jerry was grateful for such modern conveniences.

The Van Santens and Jenny were already seated in the oversized wicker chairs when Jerry ventured out onto the terrace. Moving from chair to chair and holding on to each one uncertainly like a shell-shocked soldier, he collapsed into the first vacant seat he could find.

"Well, this beats walking in the garden, doesn't it?" Ernest asked as he poured the drinks into deep crystal martini glasses. "Good booze, good neighbors, and—" he tilted his glass to Jerry, "a good old Cincinnatier. It's a shame Preston isn't here. When's he due back?"

"He didn't exactly know," Jenny answered as she accepted her drink. "Three or four days, probably."

"Then here's to him," Ernest said raising his glass in a toast. "And up St. Louis!" He took a healthy swig and looked to the others expectantly.

This was Jerry's first martini ever, but he figured he'd be able to handle it. The fact that he hated gin and couldn't stand vermouth never entered his mind. He smiled gamely and nodded to his hosts before taking a proper taste. His eyes immediately watered and he was consumed by a fit of coughing.

Audrey busied herself by spreading snacks onto the crackers and Ernest leaned close to Jenny. "If you're worrying, don't" he said while Jerry hacked away. "I speak no evil."

Jenny smiled patiently at him and patted his hand. "Now Ernest, you know there wasn't any—"

"Zounds!" Audrey shouted, interrupting Jenny and startling Jerry out of his coughing seizure. "He's got the deadly nightshade!"

Benjamin sat beneath a tall banana tree, happily examining the root structure of a small plant he'd just extricated from its pot.

"Oh, I'm sorry, Audrey," Jenny said as she jumped up to go to her son.

"Don't be silly, darling," Audrey pooh-poohed. "We can grow another."

Squatting down next to the baby, Jenny took the plant from him and tried to replace it in the moist soil as well as she could. "Can't you read?" She scolded him good-naturedly as she pointed to an imaginary sign. " 'Please don't pick the deadly nightshade!' "

To everyone's amusement, Benjamin responded with a drool. Jenny lifted him to his feet and led him on his wobble legs back to the group. But before they reached the terrace, his stroller attracted him and he broke away from his mother to grab onto the handle.

"He's a slow developer. Still moves his lips when he reads," Jerry observed. "Here, I'll get his milk."

As he reached across the table for the glass of milk, his sleeve accidentally sloshed through the onion dip.

"Whoops!" he said as he retrieved his dripping sleeve. "Terrific! I seem to have . . . entered the dip."

As everyone turned to offer advice and minister to the pressing needs of Jerry's gooey sleeve, Benjamin lifted his father's desk diary from the carryall and began to teethe on a corner of the leather cover. But he soon became bored with the taste of cowhide and dropped it to the floor—monogrammed side up. The silver letters gleamed as the track lighting from above struck highlights from the metallic imprint.

"Oh, what a shame," Audrey consoled as she offered Jerry her napkin. "Here, use this."

"Actually, this is my only good sleeve," Jerry said, still trying to make light of the embarrassing situation. He hoped nobody noticed his blush in the evening light of the terrace. "I'd better wash it off before it hardens," he said as he rose to enter the living room. "Where's the bathroom?"

"Just turn right, darling," Audrey instructed. "You can't miss it."

"Thanks," Jerry called over his shoulder. "I never missed a bathroom in my life." He wasn't watching where he was walking and stumbled over the stroller.

"Careful, kid," he admonished Benjamin and made his way toward the hall.

Due to Jerry's collision, the stroller rolled a few inches on the carpet and partially covered the diary. Safe for the moment, unless anyone should happen to look, or unless the baby should decide to take his stroller for another lap around the living room.

"He's just darling, Jenny!" Audrey gushed. "Tell Mother, where did you really meet him?"

Jenny smiled coyly over the rim of her glass.

Rounding the couch and turning down the long hallway, Jerry opened the first door on his right. A vacuum cleaner, old gift boxes and winter coats greeted him. A closet. He was about to close the door and continue his quest for a washroom when something caught his eye.

On the bottom shelf, next to a stack of shoeboxes, a small tape recorder rested beside a familiar black box. Not quite sure what to make of the coincidence, Jerry reached above him for the string to the ceiling light. There was none. After looking down the hall to verify his solitude, he stepped into the closet and struck a match.

In the sudden glare of the match, he found the box again and picked it up to look it over. The neat white lettering announced:

ELECTRONIC SURVEILLANCE CORP.
RECEIVER—J8

He was greatly disturbed by what he'd just discovered. The black receiver was the mate to the bug Danziger had planted in Jenny's apartment.

Jerry replaced the box and switched on the tape machine. Nothing. Then he rewound it and tried again. To his surprise, his own voice came from the tiny speaker. ". . . four-hour minimum, Mrs. Moore. So that would be twelve dollars plus carfare. Thirteen-seventy."

He switched the recorder off and shook out the match. In the silence and darkness of the musty closet, his heart thundered so loudly in his chest that he was afraid somebody else might hear it. Backing out of the enclosure, Jerry crossed the hall and went into the bathroom to wash his sleeve and do some quick planning. Just his luck—the toilet was dripping noisily and he could hardly hear himself think.

When he returned to the group a few minutes later, only Jenny was facing him from the terrace. Ernest and Audrey were embroiled in one of their patented arguments over which building was which in the Manhattan skyline.

Jenny smiled pleasantly when she first saw Jerry approach. But when she noticed the agitated way in which he moved, she squinted her eyes to enable her to see him better in the dim light. He was frantically signalling her that it was time to get out of there. Once he had crossed beneath the plants' indoor growth lights, she could discern his intentions. Nodding curtly, she signalled that she understood and gestured for him to join them on the terrace for the appropriate goodbyes.

Bracing himself and hoping for a graceful exit, Jerry stepped onto the terrace. "Cold water does it every time," he announced brightly as he held up his sleeve. "I learned that at my mother's knee. When it dries, there'll be nothing left but a big stain." He shot Jenny a telling glance.

Jenny chuckled and set down her drink. "I think it's time to get Benjamin to bed," she said as she slid her chair back and stood up.

"But, sweetie, we've barely started," protested Audrey, sounding suitably hurt. "Let him go pull out some more flowers."

Jenny was already starting across the terrace. "Another time. He's really tired." She stooped to pick up the baby, who was sitting on Harvey Chortles' stomach and munching a cracker. "Come on, honey. Here we go."

With her son propped on her hip, she turned back to the Van Santens. "Thanks so much, Audrey. It was lovely."

Ernest and Audrey rose and went to accompany Jenny to the door.

"I'll get the stroller," Jerry volunteered when they had passed. He bent over to pick up Harvey Chortles and set the toy in the baby seat.

Ernest had his arm around Jenny's waist. "Jenny, my love, consider this your second home while Preston's away."

"Except for tonight," Audrey laughed. "We're going to the opera."

"For some sick reason of her own," Ernest said as he kissed the baby's cheek. "Audrey actually likes Siegfried. Personally, I hate the son of a bitch—except for his hat, of course."

While the Van Santens and Jenny shared their little

joke, Jerry quietly sneaked out to the terrace. Spreading his hands apart and using them as a unit of measurement, he assessed the height of the bannister and the distance between their balcony and Jenny's next door. Then he hastily inspected the vine-covered trellis that separated the two terraces and leaned over to look at the narrow ledge that ran along the other side of the railing.

Satisfied that he'd gathered as much information as time would allow, Jerry hustled back to the stroller and started to push it into the living room. But when he took his first step, his foot hit something. Looking down and seeing that it was the diary—still where Benjamin had dropped it—he quickly fell to his knees to pick it up.

"What's your friend doing out on the terrace?" Ernest asked as he crossed the living room and approached the glass doors.

Without hesitation, Jerry slipped the diary into the carryall and leaped to his feet.

"I was just admiring the carpet," he said frantically as Ernest came up to him. "It's amazing how close they can get to real Astroturf these days."

Eyeing him warily, Ernest stood in the doorway and listened to his guest's lame excuse. The carryall swung loosely from the stroller handle, but Jerry was certain that Van Santen hadn't seen his little escapade. Accidental split-second timing had saved him once again.

"What can I say?" he asked rhetorically, holding out his hands diffidently. "I have a thing about carpets. Just love them."

He pushed down on the stroller so that the front wheels would lift over the threshold and guided the carriage through the living room.

Ernest Van Santen allowed him to pass, then folded his arms across his chest and regarded this provocative young man. His forehead furrowed with displeasure and he narrowed his eyes as he debated what to do next.

After a few seconds, he put his hands in his pockets and went to join everyone at the front door.

Jerry reached in and removed Harvey Chortles while Jenny made Benjamin comfortable in the stroller. "Thanks very much," he said as Ernest came to Audrey's side. "It was nice meeting you and your dip."

"Nice meeting you," Audrey said, thoroughly amused with Jenny's friend.

Ernest waved, but didn't offer to shake hands. "Ciao," he said.

Jenny allowed herself to be hugged one last time by Audrey. "I'll speak to you tomorrow, darling," the older woman said.

"Fine. Bye-bye."

Ernest pulled the door open and Jerry placed the talking teddy bear on the baby's lap. Then he stood aside while Jenny wheeled the stroller into the corridor. Once she'd gone by, he nodded politely to the Van Santens and left their apartment.

As the door closed behind them, Jerry stopped at the elevator and pressed the button.

"Back door," he whispered. "They're watching us. Flash your pearly whites."

Jenny smiled, still not sure what had spooked Jerry, and watched as he backed into the elevator.

"Bye-bye, Benjamin," he waved as he leaned out. "Bye, Jenny." He stepped back in and winked to her just as the door slid shut.

Before the elevator started moving, Jerry pressed the button for the twenty-first floor, one below Jenny's, and waited. As soon as it stopped and the doors opened, he ran for the stairway. Taking the steps three at a time, he burst into the service entrance and knocked sharply on Jenny's kitchen door. They had a lot to talk about.

XIX

Jenny had the door open as soon as he knocked. She was still holding Benjamin and had to step nimbly aside to avoid colliding with Jerry as he stormed into the kitchen and slammed the door. Even though things hadn't been going especially well for them, there had been a sort of comfort in Jerry's handling of each new hardship. But his aggravated condition frightened her and all her worries worked their way to the surface again.

"What is it?" she demanded. "What happened back there?"

Jerry ran to the sink and turned the faucet on, full force. He hoped the resulting noise would obscure what he had to say in case anyone was listening in.

"The receiver to our little bug is in their apartment!" he gasped as he tried to catch his breath. "They're the ones who are taping us!"

Numbly, Jenny put Benjamin down on the floor and clutched her arms around her waist. "I don't understand."

"Neither do I," Jerry said as he took her by the arm and brought her closer to the sink. "But that detective was no detective and those people next door are part of this whole deal." He could tell she wasn't willing to accept this about her friends. "Jenny, I heard the tape. I'm certain."

"Ernest and Audrey? I can't believe they'd—I mean they loved Preston and—"

"Look. I don't know what or who they really are. But things are beginning to open up." He released her. "You put Benjamin to bed. I want to go over those papers you got from Preston's office."

But she couldn't move. Her confusion and fear were so overpowering that she seemed immobilized with indecision. Jerry slapped her on the butt and the life came back to her eyes. Affected by his enthusiasm, she swooped up the baby, kissed Jerry on the cheek, and ran down the hallway.

Jerry turned off the water and paused to appreciate the wonderful woman with whom he was suffering through this bizarre ordeal. Then he went to the stroller and removed the briefcase and diary from the canvas bag. As he was about to pass into the hallway, he came face to face with the freezer.

Behind its dark, brooding door was the secret solution to all their mysteries. Jerry continued to stare at the enameled door for a few moments until, drawn by some eerie compelling presence, he felt himself inching closer and closer to the freezer. He knew he didn't want to look inside. Yet he knew that in just a matter of seconds he was going to open the door.

As if watching himself in a dream, he saw his hand reach out and grab the chrome latch. Then he felt his shoulder muscles tighten as he pulled.

The freezer door came open easily. Jerry forced himself to look. Nothing had changed. It wasn't a dream.

Fighting down his revulsion, he swung the door closed and ran, sweating, down the hallway to the master bedroom.

The awful truth within the freezer catalyzed him into positive action. It was time to make things happen.

After inspecting the room for any other listening devices the enterprising Danziger may have left behind, he dumped the contents of Preston's briefcase on the bed

He spread out the various insurance forms and booklets and opened the diary to that day's date.

Jenny tiptoed into the bedroom and whispered, "He's asleep already."

"We don't have to whisper in here. I checked. Who's Garrett Frelinghuysen?"

She thought for a moment, raising her eyebrows as she worked the name through her memory.

"I don't know," she admitted.

Jerry handed her the open diary and she read aloud from the place he indicated. "Ten-thirty—board meeting; one o'clock—lunch, Garrett Frelinghuysen; five o'clock—haircut." The name still didn't ring any bells for her.

Jerry waited until she looked up. "Preston was supposed to have lunch with him today. Have you ever heard the name before?"

Jenny shook her head and handed the book back to him.

"Now look at the opposite page," Jerry advised.

On the left-hand page was a series of numerical doodlings:

$$4 \ / \ \overline{\begin{array}{r} 187,500 \\ 750,000 \end{array}}$$

$$3 \ / \ \overline{\begin{array}{r} 250,000 \\ 750,000 \end{array}}$$

Something about it troubled Jerry. "I don't know," he said as he closed his eyes to better visualize the name. "It sounds familiar—Frelinghuysen."

Whatever it was that nagged at him about the name wasn't about to reveal itself. He opened his eyes and looked up to Jenny. He felt helpless.

"What are all those numbers?" she asked, trying to get him back on the track.

"Who knows? They could be anything." He shrugged

144

and looked at the numerals again. "Annuities or something."

Exasperated, Jerry slapped the book shut. "The one thing we want isn't written down—who he had dinner with last night." He tossed the diary aside. "That's terrific. Real helpful. And the rest of this stuff," he passed his hand over the scattered papers, "is all insurance policies. No personal notes."

He picked up a pile of pages and leafed through them, roughly throwing each one down after he examined it. "Life insurance, life insurance, life insurance, shipping insurance. Endowment, endowment, jewelry and furs floater—that belongs to Garrett Frelinghuysen." He dropped them all on the floor and moaned. "No wonder it sounded familiar. I just saw it. And the whole thing is nothing."

They could both feel the momentum of their investigation fading away.

"Pace," Jenny said.

Jerry looked up. "Huh?"

"I said, 'pace.' You know you're at your best when you're on your feet. Try it. What do we have to lose?"

Jerry smiled uncertainly, and at Jenny's insistence, rose to his feet. Slowly at first, but then with more purpose, he began to beat a path in front of the bed.

"Okay," he said as the thoughts in his muddled mind began to crystallize. "What about Ernest and Audrey? What do they do for a living?"

"Nothing," Jenny answered. She couldn't help but smile at having Jerry back to his reliable, neurotic self so quickly. "Audrey has money. I think they play the market."

Jerry was all business again. "Did you ever meet anyone named Frank Danziger at their place?"

"Uh-uh. I don't think so."

"That's probably not his real name." He looked out the window and paced his way back to her. "You'd know him if you saw him. A horribly large person with a body like a steamer trunk and a voice like a foghorn."

"Nope. Don't know him," Jenny said. "Who is he?"

"He's the detective who isn't a detective. He had a real badge, though. Can probably park anywhere he wants." He found himself staring at the briefcase: the worn handle, the pens and notepads of a man's private life.

"He could have killed Preston," Jerry mused. "Ernest could have killed him too. Maybe like this." He held up his hands to demonstrate his thoughts to Jenny.

"They're across the hall watching through the peephole, right?" When Jenny nodded, he continued. "Preston gets out of the elevator and one of them opens the door. Then comes a quick 'Hiya, Preston ol' pal, how about a nightcap?' " He sat back down on the bed. "And so it went. Maybe." He looked up to her. "If only we could figure a motive."

Jenny nudged against his knees until he parted them. Then she sat in his lap and put her arm over his shoulder.

"I still can't believe that Ernest could be involved in a murder," she said seriously.

"Then what's that tape recorder doing over there?'" She could only reply with a feeble shrug.

Lifting her gently and setting her on the bed, Jerry stood up and said, "Jenny, right now we have nothing else to believe." He hoped he could convince himself as he tried to convince her. "It explains how the killer got in when the doorman said Preston came home alone." He was about to start pacing when another piece of the puzzle fit into place. "Also, Danziger had a perfect excuse to come in here today. There *was* a broken window last night. How would he have known about it? Either he was with Ernest and heard it, or Ernest told him about it."

"Or he really is a detective," Jenny offered, playing the devil's advocate.

"Yes," Jerry signed. "Let's move right on past that

with a simple, but eloquent, 'God forbid.' " He pointed toward the Van Santen apartment. "Do they have a sleep-in maid?"

"No . . ." She wasn't sure what he was driving at.

Jerry reached across the bed and grabbed his coat. Turning it upside down, he shook it until his cassette recorder tumbled out and bounced on the mattress. Then he pulled the microphone from the inside pocket.

"Okay," he announced, "*we* are going to tape record *them!*"

Perhaps she had pushed him too far, Jenny thought. She rose and put her hand on his chest as if to hold him back.

"You mean you're going to hide that microphone in their apartment?" she asked, not sure she wanted to hear the answer.

"Uh—huh."

"But you can't," she implored.

"Why not? I have plenty of wire." Jerry took her hand and hurried her over to the phone. "Call them," he said as he handed her the receiver. "See if they're still home."

Jenny dialed the Van Santens' number and waited. After seven rings she hung up.

"No answer," she said.

"Great," Jerry said, his eyes sparkling with anticipation. "Let's do it."

He was halfway out the door when he realized she wasn't with him. "Come on!" he called.

Jenny stood by the end table, tears filling her eyes. Jerry saw her crying and came back into the room. "What's the matter?"

"I don't know." She shook her head and a tear fell onto the bedspread. "I'm scared."

"Hey, listen." He put his arms around her and sat her down on the bed. "When I was a kid my father had one word of advice for me. I've never forgotten it."

Jerry dropped his voice an octave and imitated his

father's stern counsel. "Jerome, if ever you're in serious, deep, desperate trouble—remember, God in His infinite wisdom has ordained that I'll be playing pinochle in New Jersey. And you'll have to handle the whole thing yourself."

"Are you—" Jenny sniffed. "Are you trying to make me laugh?"

"Sort of. But a smile would be okay for starters."

The faint hint of a grin crinkled across her lips. Then she smiled broadly. Jenny threw her arms around him and held on for dear life.

XX

"You call this a screwdriver?" Jerry asked as he and Jenny stepped out onto her terrace. He held up a tiny two-piece tool that he had to snap together before it even remotely resembled a screwdriver. "And this?" He flipped a flimsy tack hammer in his hand. "This must be left over from your days in the chain gang," he teased.

"What can I say? This is not the household of a handyman, er, handywoman. Handyperson?" Jenny said, caught up in the sweep of Jerry's high spirits.

They moved toward the trellis that separated the Van Santen terrace from Jenny's. Jerry put the tools and a pair of yellow Playtex Living Gloves into his outside coat pocket. Then he tapped his inside pocket to make certain the tape recorder was secure. Satisfied that he was as well equipped as he could ever be, he stepped up on an old bridge chair and put his foot through the vines and onto the first rung of the trellis. But when he put the slightest weight on the wood, it promptly snapped like a pencil and he found himself standing on the terrace again as he slipped off the bridge chair.

Jenny started to go to his aid, but he held up his hand and pulled himself together. After methodically piecing the trellis rung back together and smoothing over the ivy he'd disturbed, so as not to leave any tell-

149

tale traces, he turned back to her and snorted, "High rents! Looks like I'll have to go around it."

Gamely, he went to the low balcony rail and looked down. Twenty-two stories below, the cobblestone courtyard glistened in the dewy evening. A cab pulled up and Martin, almost too miniscule to identify from that height, opened the door. Jerry stepped back and swallowed back his fear several times. It wasn't that he was afraid of heights, but he considered twenty-two stories to be far above and beyond the normal call of duty. He began to sweat.

"Listen Jerry, if—" Jenny started to say.

"No, Jen," he shut her off. "We have no choice."

He went back to the railing and, using Jenny's shoulder for support, he gingerly stepped over with one leg. Then he forced himself to pull the other leg over and he was soon standing on the narrow ledge that bordered the terraces. Actually, only his toes were on the ledge. The heels of his shoes were standing on air; the ledge was that slender. He clasped the bannister with his hands, forearms, and elbows and bent his legs so that his knees could touch the low wall.

From this rather inelegant position, he announced in a brave, but cracking voice, "I'll be right back—if I go." He looked up instead of down. "No, I'm going. Wait. Okay, here goes."

Fighting an erupting stomach and jellied knees, he began to inch sideways along the ledge. After a moment, he was out of breath and nearly out of will. When he went to wipe the sweat from his eyes with his left hand, he almost lost his grip. One toe slipped and came free and he dangled from the bannister, clinging with one hand and the very tip of his other shoe.

Jenny shrieked and ran to him. Leaning far over the railing, she grabbed the back of his jacket and yanked with all her might. Straining against his weight and against his panicked flailing, she finally managed to get Jerry back to a reasonably steady footing. He grasped

150

the railing with his armpits and breathed heavily, the terror of his near-fall written like bad news headlines all over his face.

"Jerry, don't. It's too dangerous," Jenny begged.

"Y'see, the tricky part is somehow getting in through their French doors, which are probably locked," he winked at her halfheartedly. If he could relieve her apprehension, then at least one of them would feel assured. "Then I've got to cleverly hide the microphone and run the wire back over here so nobody will see it."

But Jenny wasn't buying it. She looked more frightened than he did. And he was scared to death.

He wiped his moistening forehead on his sleeve. "This climbing business is the easy part," he said with hollow panache. "So easy, I'm surprised even I thought of it."

Taking a deep breath that did nothing to calm his jitters and moving slowly, he said, "Piece of cake. Besides, the cobblestones would break my fall."

Jenny walked with him as he crept along the ledge, her hand on his shoulder. When he reached the trellis, she had to let go and he continued on alone, his eyes shut tight. When he felt that he'd gone far enough, he forced his eyes open and looked back to Jenny.

She was standing at the trellis, leaning over and watching.

Virtually glued to the railing, Jerry had to will himself to loosen his toehold and bring his leg up and over the top. Once that was done, he was able to persuade the rest of his body to follow and he was soon standing on the Van Santen terrace.

With no time to waste, he snapped on the Playtex gloves, rolled up the cuffs, and went to the sliding glass door. He was growing excited by the stealthy escapade of it all and, just like a proper cat burglar, he ran his fingers along the top of the door and down the sides. He didn't know what he was feeling for, but for some reason, he figured he should do it. Then he removed the tools from his pocket and inserted the screwdriver between the door handle and the doorjamb. Tapping lightly on the handle of the screwdriver, he watched for signs of the door yielding to his efforts. Nothing. When he pulled the tools away, the hammer accidentially bumped the thumb latch of the handle and the door slid open smoothly, gliding in its tracks all the way to the rubber bumper at the other end. It hadn't been locked.

Stepping into the Van Santen living room, Jerry stood by the open door and waited until his eyes became accustomed to the darkness. Then he took one step and immediately bumped into a pedestal by the piano. The ancient Egyptian vase on top wobbled and then fell. Dropping to his knees, Jerry was just able to intercept it a few inches from the floor. After setting it squarely in the center of the pedestal, he turned to his right and began to explore the room.

Before he could react, he found himself completely entangled in a tenacious jungle of banana and rubber trees. It was as if the plants had minds of their own as their tentacle-like fronds wrapped themselves around Jerry's upper body. He flailed about wildly, terrified by this unseen nightmare of clinging foliage. But then he relaxed. This audacious collection of greenery was the perfect place to hide the microphone.

Squatting down on one knee, he poked around in the dirt of the potted plants as he tried to find the right spot for the mike. But in his haphazard groping, he accidentally tripped the master switch for the indoor growth lights. Green fluorescent lights suddenly hummed to life, casting an eerie hue on the entire room. Surprised, Jerry recoiled in shock and fell back against the wall by the sun room.

His breath was coming in short, rapid gulps, and he ordered himself to calm down. Just as he was about to return to the plants, he put his hand on the wall to guide himself and inadvertently flicked the switch to Ernest's stereo. The resounding overture of Beethoven's Fifth

Symphony blared forth from powerful speakers all over the apartment. Swiping frantically at the series of switches on the wall, Jerry pushed and flicked everything he could feel

Through the incredible racket of the pumped-up orchestration, Jerry heard footsteps running through the kitchen and into the foyer. Then he heard the front door open; there was a quiet moment; then the door was slammed shut. The faint sound of footsteps retreated urgently down the corridor. And then they were gone.

The strong beam of the overhead track lighting came on as he continued to hack away at the wall switches and a tiny pinspot illuminated the papier-maché figure at the piano. Jerry shrieked at the abrupt appearance of the mad pianist and, crazed with fear, punched at every single switch within striking distance.

As suddenly as the deafening music had come on, it ceased, leaving only a reverberating echo to rattle the picture frames for a few seconds more. In the new quiet, Jerry puzzled over what he thought he'd just heard. It was difficult to be certain about the sound of the footsteps, considering the intensity of the music and the pounding in his ears.

Leaving the pinspot turned on for the time being, Jerry furtively crept back toward the center of the living room. Just as he was about to begin poking around the flower pots again, he happened to glance at the couch. This time a low, guttural scream escaped his lips before he could stifle himself.

It was Ernest Van Santen.

But Mr. Van Santen was lying sprawled face-down across the end of the couch with a long kitchen knife sticking straight up from the center of his back. Dapper to the last, he was dressed in a white tuxedo, the back of which was gradually turning the color of his deep red carnation as his blood ebbed through the wound and trickled between the cushions of the couch.

With the microphone dangling uselessly in his gloved

hands, Jerry stood rooted to the spot. He could feel another scream boiling its way up his throat as his eyes bulged with panic.

With considerable effort, he managed to pry his feet from the carpet and get them moving again. He started to go to Ernest's body to see if he were still alive, but the glazed stare on Van Santen's horribly shocked face left no doubt. The man was very dead.

Jerry whirled and started for the terrace, but then he remembered the footsteps he thought he had heard. Now he *knew* he'd heard them. The murderer might come back. Spinning on his heel, he ran to the foyer to bolt and chain the front door. He was vaguely conscious of the sound of dripping water coming from down the hall as he slipped the chain into its slot.

That's when he saw her.

Audrey Van Santen was slumped across the long dining room table. Another long kitchen knife protruded from the back of her chic black satin gown. Her blood formed a thick pool on the table and dripped, rhythmically as rain, onto the white carpet beneath her. She still clutched her pearl purse in her left hand.

Jerry had seen enough. His hair flying, he tore across the foyer, through the living room and out onto the terrace. Turning hard on one leg, he ran to the trellis and wildly tore at the vines.

"What happened in there?" Jenny asked from the other side.

"They're dead," he shrieked hysterically.

"Dead?"

"Both of them!" he shouted as he continued to rip the ivy from the trellis. "They're lying in there with big knives sticking in them—"

Jenny turned away. "Oh, God. No—"

"Completely killed!" he went on, working himself into a frenzy of irrationality. "I can't believe it. Go make plans to listen to an opera these days and see what it gets you. I mean, they're dead! Totally!"

154

Jenny got the point. "Come back over here," she pleaded as she looked at him through the bare spot in the trellis. "Jerry, please."

But Jerry wasn't finished ranting yet. "There's a maniac loose! I heard him running out of there. Jesus Christ!" He smacked himself on the forehead with the palm of his Playtex Living Glove. "I just realized I have to go back in and get the tape they made of us."

Doing exactly what he didn't want to do, he turned and started back for the Van Santens' door.

Clinging to the wooden slats of the trellis, Jenny cried out, "Jerry—don't!"

He stopped and turned to look at her. "Get Benjamin dressed!" he commanded, making absolutely certain she understood how critical it was that she comply. "We're getting out of here. Hurry!" Then he spun around and ran to the Van Santens' terrace door.

Jenny watched him go into the other apartment. Then she bolted into her own living room and ran for the baby's room.

Doing everything possible to avoid looking at Ernest's body in the unsettling green glow of the plant lights, Jerry stayed close to the piano on the left side of the room as he crossed toward the hall. The long microphone wire swung in a wide arc as he walked.

Turning down the hallway, he hurriedly opened the closet door and reached inside. Something very heavy fell across his arms and Jerry toppled into the closet and became ensnared in some loudly rattling obstacle. Punching and kicking his way back out of the closet, he flung whatever it was to the floor and scooted across the hall to the bathroom. With his eyes still glued on the closet floor, he swept his hand along the bathroom wall and turned on the light. He had been attacked by a bag of golf clubs.

Having long since lost his composure, Jerry was in imminent danger of losing his dinner. Puffing out his cheeks and holding his stomach, he lurched to the drip-

155

ping toilet and lifted the seat. He stood there for a full minute, crouched over with his hands on his knees, gagging and trying to make something happen. But it was no use.

He waited another few seconds and then straightened up gasping.

"When it's really crucial," he moaned to himself, "I can never throw up. I just have no luck."

Disgusted, he turned to leave the bathroom. But the microphone cord had looped itself around the handle of the toilet and, when Jerry gave it a tug, the toilet began to flush loudly. He unhooked the wire and darted across the hall.

Illuminated by the bathroom light, the Van Santens' tape recorder was easily discernible on the bottom shelf of the closet. Jerry stepped over the golf bag, grabbed both reels, and ripped the tape from the machine. He was about to tear back down the hallway when he realized that the troublesome toilet was still flushing noisily.

Shaking his head at yet another improbable inconvenience, Jerry ran back into the bathroom and jiggled the handle. It continued to flush. If he left it alone, he knew the neighbors were bound to complain. He took the Kleenex box and hand towel display from the top of the toilet and removed the procelain cover.

As he peered into the bubbling tank to find whatever was causing the problem, he noticed something irregular. A large, clear, plastic bag was taped to the inside wall of the tank. Moving quickly, Jerry reached in and tore it out. When he held the bag up to inspect it in the light, he let out a low whistle of amazement.

It was filled with jewelry. Diamond rings and necklaces, loose rubies, emeralds, and other stones, gold watches, and silver pins, all sparkled brilliantly before him. A trickle of water streamed down from the wet bag and was efficiently captured in the upturned cuff of his rubber glove. Distracted from this unexpected treasure by the persistent flushing of the toilet, Jerry gave the tank a swift kick to the midsection. To his surprise, the toilet sputtered and then stopped bubbling altogether. After taking time to stare at the considerable cache in his hands, he scooped up the recording tape and whizzed down the hallway.

He hit the terrace like a madman, the jewelry, microphone, long cord, screwdriver, hammer, and recording tape all cuddled in his arms. Without a second thought, he lowered his head like a charging bull and leaped through the flimsy trellis, splintering it like a house of Popsicle sticks.

Rolling over once, Jerry bounded to his feet and burst into Jenny's apartment. She stood by the fireplace with the baby in her arms. She knew better than to ask any questions just then.

XXI

Jerry could hear Mrs. Calamesa snooping around behind her door as he and Jenny huddled in the lower hallway of his building and rearranged their packages. Propping Benjamin high on his waist and grabbing up a bag of groceries, Jerry ignored his meddlesome landlady and started up the stairs. Jenny tucked a small suitcase full of clothes for her and the baby under one arm and lifted another bag full of Benjamin's toys and Preston's briefcase with the other. With the caterpillar's antennae bobbing and Harvey Chortles staring ahead mutely from her arms, she followed Jerry up the stairs.

When they finally reached Jerry's floor, everyone was out of breath except Benjamin. Putting down the groceries, Jerry opened the door, kicked the *New York Times* inside, and entered his flat. After he switched on a few lights and gave the place a cursory once-over glance, he went back to retrieve the groceries and ushered Jenny into his home.

Half an hour later, Benjamin was sound asleep on Jerrys bed. Almost every chair in the apartment was propped against the bed to prevent him from falling off. But he was sleepng so deeply that they had little worry about him stirring.

Busy in the kitchen, Jenny had changed into a red plaid flannel shirt and slate-grey slacks tucked into high, brown boots. She'd pinned her hair up and rolled up her sleeves so that she could prepare something for them to eat. Grabbing a tray of wine, provolone cheese, anchovies, and French bread, she came into the front room where Jerry was hunched over his desk.

While Jenny made their favorite sandwiches, Jerry puzzled over the astouding array of jewelry spread out before him. On the floor next to his chair, Preston's datebook was propped up against his briefcase.

After accepting a glass of wine, Jerry held a dazzling diamond choker and asked incredulously, "Is it real?" It was too beautiful to be otherwise. "That's a stupid question," he scoffed. "Who hides fake jewelry in a toilet?"

Perplexed by yet another confounding development in an already impossible situation, Jerry rubbed his eyes and held his head in his hands. Jenny stood behind him and kneaded the taut muscles of his shoulders and neck.

"This stuff's obviously stolen," he said as he drove himself to stay alert. "And it's got to be the reason why this maniac is constantly putting knives into people." He stretched and took Jenny's hands in his. "Okay. It's either stolen from a better-type store or from a sickeningly rich person." He leaned back and looked up to her. "So what was it doing hidden in Ernest and Audrey's gurgling toilet?"

Jenny pecked him on the nose and went back to the sandwiches. "They stole it?" she conjectured. "Is that what you're driving at?"

That was precisely what Jerry had in mind.

"With Frank Danziger. I think that's what I'm saying." He put a few anchovies into the sandwich Jenny offered him and held it over the table, shaking it in punctuation as he began to piece together the complicated puzzle.

"Okay. Let's see where this takes us," he began. "Ernest and Audrey probably spent half their waking lives at parties thrown by the rich and very rich. Mr. and Mrs. Chic. Really fun people. Very much in demand.

Right?" He thrust the French bread toward Jenny in emphasis.

"I guess that's a good description," she agreed as she pushed the sandwich back to him. "Right."

"So they knew the layouts of all those loaded apartments and they planned the robberies. And Danziger, your average Mr. Muscle, carried them out." He ripped a huge bite from the sandwich. After chewing for a while, he continued enthusiastically. "Or maybe they did it together. However, it doesn't matter." He swallowed and took another bite, eating with an appetite that surprised him. "And Ernest and Audrey kept the loot until they could do whatever you do with this stuff. How does that sound to you?"

Jenny looked up and stopped picking at the cheese that reached beyond the edges of her sandwich. "What about Preston?"

"I was just about to ask *you* that," Jerry sighed.

He picked up his wine glass in one hand and, with his food in the other, rose to begin pacing around the table.

"What about Preston?" he mused. "Somehow he found out about the whole operation and—" They both knew that wouldn't do it. "Doesn't figure, does it?" he asked.

His pacing brought him to the small chair by the front door. It was filled with an overflowing pile of the *New York Times*. Jerry stood facing the chair and the papers, knowing that somehow they could provide the missing clue. He reached out and touched the top paper and held his hand on it for a few seconds, as if trying to divine the secrets it held. Then he looked at the jewels on the table and he grew excited. He put his wine and sandwich down on the floor.

"Hey!" he yelled as he scooped up the papers and brought them toward the table. "Start looking through these!" He let them go and they tumbled to the floor at Jenny's feet.

They both sat crosslegged and attacked the stack of

newspapers. "I save them all week and absorb the total cumulative shock on Sunday mornings when I can lie down." They rustled through the pages as fast as they could.

"We're looking for a big jewel heist, right?" Jenny asked as she threw one section down and went to work on another.

Jerry nodded without looking up. He turned a page, read something, and said, "Shit!" Then he threw the paper aside disgustedly.

"What? What did you find?"

"Oh, nothing," he said sheepishly. "It's just—uh, the Jets lost—"

Jenny smiled and they both dove back into the papers. Jerry tossed away the classified, sports, home, and entertainment sections and passed the hard news and society pages to Jenny.

Fifteen minutes later, their fingers were black from the newsprint and they only had a few more pages to leaf through.

Jenny picked up another section and scanned the front page. An article at the bottom attracted her attention and she read it quickly. "Here!" she exclaimed triumphantly.

"Where?" Jerry asked wearily, almost ready to give up this torturous scheme.

"Last Monday," Jenny said as she read the headline. *$1,500,000 Jewel Theft.*"

Raising himself to his knees, Jerry eyed the jewelry that lay glittering under the drafting lamp. "Is that stuff worth a million and a half dollars?"

"Listen," Jenny shushed him as she continued reading. " 'Masked intruders made off with over one and a half million dollars worth of jewelry in a daring early evening raid on the East Side townhouse of financier—" She looked up at Jerry, her eyes bright. "—Garrett Frelinghuysen."

"Frelinghuysen!" Jerry clapped his hands and

jumped to his feet as he proclaimed, "A name never to be forgotten!"

He grabbed up Preston's briefcase, popped it open and dumped the papers and policies on the floor. Then he dropped to his knees, and hands flat and racing, he ruffled through the paperwork until he found what he wanted.

"Got it!" he declared as he held up a thick policy. "Garrett Frelinghuysen. Jewelry and fur floater." Sitting down on the floor again, he swiftly riffled through the pages. "Twenty-six carat, square-cut, blue-white diamond ring—diamond pendant—ruby necklace—Emerald choker—that could be painful—" He reached the last page. "It's all here!"

Dropping the policy back into the briefcase, he picked up Preston's diary and flipped through the pages. "And Preston was supposed to have lunch with him today!" But then he realized that somehow it didn't make any sense and his shoulders sagged. "It still doesn't figure," he groaned as he let the datebook slip from his fingers.

Jenny chewed methodically on her bottom lip. Ordinarily she would have gone to Jerry to comfort him, to offer support, to recommend that he pace. But she was working on a theory of her own. She was searching her memory for something she knew was there, the elusive key to the entire mystery.

"Wait! It does make sense," she almost shouted. Her eyes gleamed as she leaned forward and energetically told Jerry what she had remembered. "I think I know how it all fits together!" She took a deep breath and gestured animatedly with her hands as she spoke.

"Preston told me several times in the last year that his company made private deals to have stolen jewelry returned to its clients by paying the thieves half the insured value." She paused to let Jerry stew on this, but he didn't want to wait.

"Yeah, yeah, go on."

162

"And it's all done very quietly. Without involving the police," she related. "It saves the—company—money." Her mood changed abruptly and she averted her eyes. "He was very—proud of that."

Upset now, she could feel her temples grow warm and the tears beginning to work their way to the surface. Jenny was ashamed that her Preston had been involved in all that thievery and deceit.

Flipping through the pages of the diary, Jerry stopped at the page on which they'd discovered the confusing numbers. He spoke in a hushed, delicate voice, tuned in to Jenny's altered mood.

"And he was the company man who briefed Ernest and Audrey, or whomever, on which client had what jewelry and where." It was all falling into place. "And then made the deals for payments after the jewelry was stolen. In return for a cut of the money."

After pausing to examine the figures in Preston's book under this new light, he handed it to Jenny. "Look at these numbers."

Sniffing back the tears, she accepted the book and studied the numbers as he spoke:

$$4 \overline{\smash{\big)}\ 750,000} \quad 187,500$$

$$3 \overline{\smash{\big)}\ 750,000} \quad 250,000$$

"One and a half million dollars worth of jewelry is stolen," Jerry began after Jenny looked up. "The company is willing to pay half to get it back. That's seven hundred and fifty thousand." He pointed to the page. "There it is, divided into four shares. Ernest, Audrey, Danziger, and—" They exchanged a knowing look over what surely was the truth. "And Preston."

Jerry rose to his feet and stood over the table. He picked up the largest diamond necklace and twisted the drafting lamp so that it shone directly through it. A rainbow of tiny prisms danced throughout the stone. Beautiful, elegant and deadly.

"Maybe Preston was demanding a third instead of a quarter and they killed him for it." He dropped the necklace onto the heap of jewelry and sat on the chair facing Jenny. "And then Danziger killed the Van Santens because this last haul was a gem, pardon the pun, and he wanted it all to himself. And I surprised him while he was trying to find the stuff."

When he looked at Jenny, she seemed terribly alone, very small, in the middle of the floor. He stepped over the newspapers and the rest of the debris from their investigation and held out his hands to her. As she accepted his hands and pulled herself up, he continued to puzzle over the motive.

"The only thing is, why would they kill Preston to begin with? He was their middle man." Jenny wrapped her arms around him while he spoke. "It makes sense, and it doesn't make sense. So it's true to life, right?"

She answered with a demanding, desperate hug.

Sensing the urgency in her embrace, Jerry walked her over to the dilapidated green couch and coaxed her to lie down. "A girl could get lost in there," he cautioned lightly.

She grabbed his hair and pulled him close. "I'll take my chances," she whispered.

Jenny maneuvered her weight to the rear of the couch to make room for Jerry. He kicked off his shoes and lay down beside her. Then he pulled the old wool blanket down from the back of the couch and covered both of them. Jenny lifted her head to allow him to put his left arm underneath her neck. Then she took his right hand and kissed his fingers.

Running her tongue up and down the length of his index finger, she pressed her body close to his. When she turned to kiss him on the mouth, she realized that he was just lying there, staring at the ceiling.

"What's the matter?" she asked, concerned.

"Nothing. I'm just thinking," he answered without turning.

"About what?"

Jerry blew out a long, controlled breath and shifted around to face her. "Jenny, I think I have a plan that is so insane I hesitate to admit that I even thought of it." He waited for her response, and when she nodded to indicate she was willing to hear him out, he continued.

"The only one left in this thing is Danziger, and that's obviously not his name, so we have no way of finding him without my risking my life—which is part of the plan."

Jerry had anticipated her objection and held a finger to her lips before she could say anything.

"No, wait. Let me finish," he said. "Likewise, he has no way of finding us."

Jenny took his finger away from her mouth and said, "Ernest and Audrey knew your last name. If they told it to him, all he has to do is look it up in the phone book."

"I'm not listed. In New York the heavy breathers call guys too. So you and Benjamin are safe here." He put his hand on her shoulder and let his fingers pass over the arm of her red flannel shirt. He squeezed and felt the firm muscles in her slender arm. Jenny threw her leg over his hip and nibbled on his earlobe.

"Okay," he said, pulling himself away from her distractions. "Somebody's going to start discovering bodies pretty soon, so I can't waste any time. And neither can Danziger. If he wants that jewelry, he's got to go back to the Van Santens' place to look for it. Now, according to this plan—"

Jenny flicked her tongue behind his ear and cooed, "Let's make plans in the morning, okay?" She pressed her thighs against his and began unbuttoning his shirt.

Turning onto his side, Jerry held her close and touched his tongue to the tip of her nose. Then they kissed. A deep, searching, probing kiss. As they caressed, Jerry put his hand lightly, tentatively on her breast. Jenny pushed her body closer to his.

Their tongues touching and teasing sweetly, Jerry began to unbutton her shirt. She shifted her body to make it easier for him and he slipped his hand inside.

Without breaking off the kiss, he whispered into her mouth, his lips moving against hers, "Uh, my arm fell asleep." They parted from each other a fraction of an inch. "God only knows where the blood went."

Rising up on her elbow, Jenny smiled and said, "My turn." She put her right arm under his neck and allowed him to have both hands free.

They kissed again, tenderly, comfortable with each other. His hand gently explored her body, learning, discovering the exquisite contours.

"The pins and needles just started," Jerry laughed as he shook his left arm.

"Good. That rules out gangrene." She smiled and bit his nose.

"You're beginning to sound like me," he said and pinched her, playfully. He leaned in to kiss her again, but stopped abruptly and mused, "You know, in the midst of all this terror, I just thought of something really terrifying."

"What?" Jenny asked, amused.

"Suppose you'd stayed in Cincinnati for the rest of your life?"

"Don't ever say that again," Jenny cautioned soberly. Then she wrapped both her arms around him and brought her body beneath his until he was lying on top of her. "Let's talk about how happy I am that we're together."

She grabbed a handful of his hair and kissed him hard and full on the mouth. Needing no further urging from her, Jerry removed his shirt and dropped it on the floor. Then he slipped her shirt down her back and pulled the blanket up to their shoulders.

And there, in an attic apartment in Greenwich Village, on a creaky secondhand couch, exhausted by the uncanny events of the previous two days, unsure of what the next day would bring—time stopped for them. And Jenny Moore and Jerry Green made love for the first time.

XVII

XXII

At eight the next morning, the sunlight was already streaming into Jerry's apartment. Although it was November, the day dawned clear and warm. Jerry had risen first, reluctantly separating himself from the sweet tangle of Jenny's arms and legs. She stirred, muttered something, and rolled over to go back to sleep.

Pulling open the drapes, Jerry stood by the window and admired Jenny as the early light flooded the room. Then, while he showered and dressed for work, Jenny awoke and went into the bedroom to tend to Benjamin.

She was sitting at the desk, cradling the baby and feeding him his formula, when Jerry came down the hall, a blue tie thrown loosely around his neck and a grey tweed sport coat over his arm.

Jenny lifted her face for Jerry's kiss and smiled warmly. They were in love and they let the happiness in their eyes do the talking. Tossing his coat over the back of a chair, Jerry took Harvey Chortles from the grocery bag and laid it face-down on the table.

"Put the jewels back in the plastic bag, would you, Jen?" he asked.

While Jenny scooped up the jewelry, Jerry took a single-edged razor blade, and carefully lining up his incision like a surgeon, sliced a long, straight cut in the back of the toy. Slipping his hand into the hole, he plucked out the voice mechanism and severed the thin wires with the blade.

"Thanks" he muttered when Jenny slid the bag of jewels over to him. "Now, please thread that needle," he said, pointing to a spool of brown thread with a large needle stuck in its side.

Then he carefully laid the jewels inside Harvey Chortles and rearranged some of the stuffing to keep them secure.

"Trade?" he asked, and held the teddy bear out to Jenny. She handed over the baby, who eagerly went to Jerry's outstretched arms, and began sewing the back of the toy.

"Benjamin," he said seriously, "I swear I'll make this up to you."

When Jenny finished and snapped off the thread, Jerry put the teddy bear into a bag. Then he grabbed up his coat and said, "Don't worry," as he kissed Jenny goodbye.

He closed the door softly and left Jenny sitting at the table, worried and frightened about his latest plan.

On his way to Macy's, Jerry took the subway one stop farther than necessary. When he emerged from the underground tunnel, he stepped into the phone booth by the newsstand and quickly jotted down the number of the telephone.

It was long before opening time when he got to the employees' entrance. He pounded on the door for a full two minutes before Cappy, the night watchman, could be aroused from his sleep at his watch station.

Cappy was an old Macy's employee, long since put out to pasture by mandatory retirement. But he was an energetic sort and had gone to a security guard agency training school for six months. The sympathetic Macy's administration relented and brought him back on the night security patrol.

When he saw Jerry through the door's window, his

craggy face warmed into a smile. "Hiya, Jerry," he greeted him. "What are you doing in so early?"

Jerry shifted the paper bag to his left hand and slapped his old friend on the back. "Hey Cap. How're you doing?" he said brightly. "I'm, uh, sort of lobbying for daylight savings time to come back."

Cappy grunted in confused laughter, the humor of Jerry's quick wit benignly passing him by.

"Seriously, Cap. I came to go over my books," Jerry said as he led him back to his watch station. "You better get back to your beauty sleep or the boss'll think something's wrong." He passed through the swinging doors and called over his shoulder, "See you later, pal."

Moving quickly through the main floor of the store, Jerry passed the cosmetics and foundations department and headed for the front of the store. He checked his watch. The first wave of employees would be arriving any minute and he had to hurry.

He reached the famous Macy's window displays that lined the entire front wall of the store. Peeking into each one while trying not to be seen from the street, he finally came to the one he wanted. Crouching low, he pulled Harvey Chortles from the paper bag and yanked open the door of the *Bambini* window display. Then he deftly grabbed an identical Harvey Chortles from its place on a miniature swing and replaced it with the teddy bear with the jeweled treasure inside.

After he closed the doors and put the innocent Harvey Chortles into his bag, he stood up and ran for the rear of the store. Bursting through the fire door, he tore up the two flights of stairs to his floor. He threw the Harvey Chortles from the downstairs window onto a pile of stuffed animals at Helene's counter. Then he hurried across to his own department and began to fill the bag with things that he'd need to begin the next stage of his plan.

A light blond mustache, sideburns, and goatee beard, fake glasses, and a dark felt homburg hat were tossed into the bag in a matter of seconds. Running over to the counter by the elevators, Jerry grabbed up a black, simulated leather doctor's satchel and added it to his hoard. Then, after pausing to think whether he had forgotten anything, he burst through the fire door again and flew down the stairs.

Cappy was snoring too loudly to be disturbed when Jerry whisked by, scurrying down the corridor and out to the street.

XXIII

When Wayland first saw the man approaching, he figured that he seemed too young for the old-fashioned muttonchop sideburns and goatee. Then he noticed the black medical bag the man was carrying and somehow that made everything seem proper.

"Good morning, sir. Can I help you?" Wayland said pleasantly when the well-dressed young man reached the door.

"Yes. I'm Dr. Robertson," Jerry said in a faintly English accent, as he tipped the brim of his homburg in greeting. "I'm Mr. Moore's physician. He's expecting me."

"Oh, yeah," Wayland said as he held the door open for the good doctor. "Got the flu, huh?" He picked up the house phone and prepared to dial the Moore's number.

"Yes. Yes, he's got the flu," Jerry concurred as he crossed the lobby and headed for the elevators. "So I'll go right up because this is a house call." He smiled sweetly and stepped into the waiting elevator car.

Wayland thought about how silly the doctor looked in that ugly beard and returned the phone to its cradle.

As soon as Jerry had let himself into Jenny's apartment, he hurried across the living room and out onto the terrace. He dropped the doctor's bag and pulled two sheets of paper from his inside coat pocket. Each was identical and he carefully double-checked the message he'd pasted on them with letters and words cut out of his newspapers.

Below the Macy's Department Store logo, he'd painstakingly prepared the message: *INFORMATION REGARDING JEWELRY AVAILABLE MACY'S TOY DEPARTMENT TODAY ONLY AFTER 2 P.M. WEAR A BERET.*

Rolling the pages and holding them in his left hand, he climbed up on the bridge chair and eased himself through the huge hole he'd torn in the trellis when he crashed through the night before. Once he was on the Van Santen terrace, he crept lightly toward their sliding glass doors and peeked inside.

Essentially, the living room appeared to be exactly the same way he held it when he had so unceremoniously run for his life the previous evening. Ernest Van Santen lay in deathly repose on the couch, a little stiffer perhaps, but undisturbed.

Straining to keep from looking at the ghastly sight of Ernest's body, Jerry passed into the room and sidled over to the piano. The mad pianist was poised as ever, his arched fingers hovering over the keyboard. After propping one of the pasted-up messages against the papier-maché musician, Jerry stepped back to get a better perspective on how it looked. After he was convinced that it was emminently noticeable, he turned around and started for the foyer.

That was when he saw Danziger.

Frank Danziger, bogus detective, lay flopped over the bar in the sun room. Predictably, a long kitchen knife was sticking out of his back, just a little left of center. His face was frozen in a tortured death scream.

In spite of himself, Jerry let out a piercing "Yow!" and backed clumsily into the piano. Tearing his eyes away from the latest victim, he gathered his wits about him momentarily and ran to the Van Santens' foyer. Absolutely refusing to look into the dining room and

173

risking the discovery of any other corpses besides Audrey, he impaled the other message on a protrusion of one of the expensive sculptures by the door and barreled back through the living room.

But he involuntarily hesitated and stole another masochistic glance at Danziger's body. At that moment, there came a resounding crash from somewhere in the back of the apartment, followed by the sound of footsteps running down the hallway.

Without even bothering to turn in the direction of the noise, Jerry streaked out the door, dove through the trellis, did a double roll and came up running into Jenny's living room.

When he reached the downstairs lobby, obviously harried and sweating, he bustled toward the doorman and gestured impatiently for him to open the door.

"How's Mr. Moore?" Wayland asked.

"Stand back!" Jerry shouted. "I'm covered with germs."

Just as Jerry jumped into a standing taxi in the courtyard, twenty-two stories below, the mad pianist had a visitor. A gloved hand picked up the cryptic message, hesitated, then angrily crumpled it into a ball.

XXIV

Just barely arriving at work on time, Jerry punched in and made a beeline for the employees' washroom. As soon as he was alone, he pulled the various disguises from his pocket and stuffed them deep into the waste basket. Then he scrubbed the remainder of the glue from his lip and chin and left the room just as his supervisor came in carrying the *DAILY NEWS*.

Now that he knew exactly where his boss was, and observing that he would be in there for some time catching up on his reading, Jerry felt safe enough to call Jenny. He put a dime in the pay phone in the corridor and dialed his number.

She answered on the first ring.

"Jenny?" Jerry said, somehow calming now that he'd heard her voice.

"So far everything's going fine—except for one item of interest."

Jenny was standing in the middle of Jerry's living room, with the phone in her hand. "What item is that?" she asked sweetly as she watched Benjamin tussle with the caterpillar.

"Are you sitting down?" Jerry asked. "Frank Danziger is lying there beside Ernest with a big knife sticking out of his back." He smashed his fist into the wall in frustration. "It's like a new fad or something!"

The color drained from Jenny's face and she collapsed onto the couch.

"Jenny, did you hear me?"

"Yeah," she said hollowly, stunned at yet another murder. She had just started to allow herself to feel the tiniest semblance of hope. And now this.

Two men from the accounting department walked by; Jerry held his hand over the mouthpiece as he spoke. "So we have an entirely new maniac on our hands. We don't know who the hell he is, and my note is sitting up there in Ernest and Audrey's apartment." The washroom door opened and he quickly turned his back. "I think maybe we're in trouble."

Jenny sat forward on the couch and spoke very slowly, measuring each word carefully. "Jerry, we've got to call the police *now*. There's just no other—"

"We can't! They'll think I killed Danziger!" he interrupted her impatiently. His supervisor was coming his way and he knew he only had a few seconds to finish the call. "I'll call you back. I love you. Don't leave my place. Lock everything in sight. How's Benjamin?"

Without waiting for a reply, he slipped the receiver back onto the phone and stared at the wall forlornly. He nodded curtly to his supervisor and started for his department. When he reached the floor, he spotted Helene heading directly for him and it was apparent from the intent way she was walking that something was on her mind. And he knew that something was him.

But he had too much on his mind to deal with her. Remembering that the best defense was a hardhitting offense, he started jabbering before she could get within striking distance.

"The dentist gave me such a shot of novocaine that I'm numb from my lip to my hip," he mumbled out of the side of his mouth as he twisted his face in mock agony. "Total gum replacement after lunch!"

And he fled past her for the sanctuary of his familiar counter. After making certain that Helene was not giving chase, he stepped behind his display case and pretended to be busy for a few moments. Then, when he was positive no one was looking, he pulled four envelopes from his coat pocket.

Inspecting them for the thousandth time, he checked again that each was numbered one through four consecutively and they were indeed in the proper order. Then he checked his watch, and as his thoughts carried him drifting away, he absently tapped the envelopes against his palm.

"Are you the salesperson here?"

Jerry jumped at the thundering voice and thrust the envelopes inside his coat. Then he turned to face what he was sure was going to be a longshoreman or an angry marine. But he was surprised to see a woman no more than five feet tall peering over the top of the counter.

She had the body of a tractor tire and the sense of humor of a runaway slave.

"Can I help you, madam?" Jerry offered as he switched on his Macy's personality.

"That *is* what you're here for, isn't it?" she bellowed in what, for her, was probably a whisper. "Do you sell machine guns?"

"No, we don't, madam. Try the Pentagon or the PLO." And he brusquely turned away, looking for other customers. "Next!" he called to the nonexistent crowd.

The dwarfish shrew stood there with her mouth dropped open in indignation. But as Jerry continued to ignore her, she had no choice but to stomp off in search of other departments to terrorize.

XXV

Much to the delight of the Manhattan lunch crowd, the day continued to grow unseasonably warmer. Jerry punched out at exactly twelve-thirty and hurried from Macy's. He strode quickly uptown through the pressing foot traffic, crossing against the lights and dodging taxi cabs. At 59th Street, he skipped through the line of standing limousines in front of the Plaza and scooted across to Central Park.

An old man with a pushcart was peddling steamed hot dogs beneath a faded umbrella. Jerry bought one, hastily scraped some mustard along the bun, and entered the Park. Munching the hot dog in huge bites, he walked directly down the center of the asphalt path. Pigeons scattered at his approach and fled to watch him from atop discolored statues of heroes and horses. Street people clamored for handouts and pushers did their hustle, but Jerry continued on.

When he came to the vast series of green park benches that marked the Mall, he paused to glance around. Tossing the wrapper from his hot dog into a wire trash basket, Jerry sat on a bench in the first row and looked up at the band shell. Some kids were carousing on skateboards, the buzz of their wheels echoing out over the benches. After another few moments of watching the kids and their mayhem, Jerry rose and walked deeper into the series of benches. Counting each row as he went, he stopped at the seventh row and sat on the first bench.

Trying to appear nonchalant, he slipped his hand into his coat and removed the four envelopes. Then he chose the one marked *#1* and returned the other three to his pocket. After pulling a precut piece of Scotch tape off his belt, he secured the tape to the back of the envelope and looked over his shoulder. Convinced that he had so far remained unseen, he quickly bent forward as if to tie his shoe and stuck the envelope securely to the underside of the bench.

Although he was wearing loafers, he continued the shoe-tying charade to its logical conclusion.

After pretending to double-knot the invisible laces, he stood up slowly and made his way back down the rows again. When he reached the band shell, he turned to his right and headed for the Bethesda Fountain restaurant.

A few businessmen and well-dressed ladies in their autumn hats were at the patio tables, talking their lunchtime away. Just as Jerry hoped, the table closest to the busboys' station was still vacant. Seating himself and picking up a discarded sports section from a nearby chair, he scrutinized the other diners.

Once he determined that it was safe, he reached into his jacket and removed the envelope marked *#2*. Repeating the Scotch tape procedure, he surreptitiously fastened the envelope to the bottom of the table. Having done this, he rose and headed back toward the main pathway just as a busboy came over with place settings for his table.

While Jerry watched from a short distance, the busboy set four places at the table in one blurry, skilled motion that took less than ten seconds. Then he went off to clean another table. The envelope was left undisturbed.

The kindergarten kids were out in full force at the playground. Young mothers and an occasional father sat on benches while they supervised, or stood in the sand and pushed their offspring skyward on sturdy swings.

Jerry sidled up to the railing near the three metal slides. A line of children squeaked and squealed their way down the smooth steel, bumped their butts on the rubber padding and jumped up to do it again. After waiting patiently for almost fifteen minutes, there was a lull in the energies of the happy kids and Jerry stepped over the railing.

Stooping over to shake a pebble out of his shoe, he slapped the *#3* envelope beneath the ramp of the middle slide. Then, fumbling with his loafer, he hopped back to one of the other slides and sat down to put his shoe back on.

"Watch it, Mister!" came a strident voice, and before Jerry could react, a four-year-old Puerto Rican girl plowed into his backside.

Jerry jumped up to apologize to the child, but she turned away and ran back to the ladder for another try at him.

His lunch hour was just about over and Jerry didn't have the time or the inclination to lose any battles to a feisty little brat. He stuck out his tongue at the urchin and hurried back to Macy's.

XXVI

The pattern of Jerry's lifestyle that day was such that he lived for lunchtime and coffee breaks. He'd become a skittish clock watcher. Through some peculiar quirk, Macy's was exceptionally busy, much busier than its usual late-afternoon rush and he was being run ragged by a feverish pre-Christmas crowd.

As soon as his five o'clock break came around, he handed his order book over to one of the part-time help and worked his way through the shoppers toward the pay phone. Once there, he dropped in a dime and dialed the number of his apartment. There was no answer. After letting it ring twenty times, hoping to catch Jenny napping or just walking in, he hung up and leaned his head against the wall.

He'd specifically told her to stay home. Now she was gone and he was uneasy, not knowing where she was.

When he emerged from the employees' area, Helene was gesturing from her counter for him to come over. But he ignored her, as had become his custom, and made his way over to the escalators. Frantic over the whereabouts of Jenny, he stepped onto the top step of the down escalator. But it was moving too slowly to suit him, so he nudged his way past the shoppers and began to scurry down the moving stairway. He was becoming increasingly obsessed with finding Jenny.

From her vantage point behind her counter, Helene

peered through her customers to watch Jerry as he shoved his way past the other customers on the escalator.

Suddenly, he stopped dead in his tracks. There, on the up escalator right next to him was a man wearing a beret. The man was stocky, in his late forties, and dressed in a rumpled black suit with an open black shirt. A cigarette dangled from his lips and he had a week's growth of grey stubble on his chin. He stared straight ahead and narrowed his light blue eyes as he approached the third floor.

Jerry stood spellbound as the man was carried past him. Then he turned and started to push his way back up the down escalator. Clambering like a madman, he bulled his way past the same shoppers he'd battered on the way down.

He burst free at the top of the stairs and slowed to what he hoped would appear to be a somewhat inconspicuous pace. All the while keeping a watchful eye on the man with the beret, he made his way toward his counter on the far wall.

Because Jerry wasn't watching where he was going, he bumped sharply into the corner of his counter. The entire case jiggled from the impact and the row of customers looked up as he rubbed his hip and smiled stupidly. Then, still straining to watch the mysterious man, he went around behind the display and stood next to the costume rack.

The man with the beret idled his way through the sporting goods section, cursorily looking over the equipment. After a few seconds at one display, he moved over to another and spend a couple of moments inspecting the merchandise there.

Passing from the sporting goods department to the camping section, he passed over most of the outdoor displays and paid only mild attention to the tent and sleeping bag setups. He took the cigarette butt from his mouth and lit a fresh one with it before dropping the butt on the floor and grinding it out with his heel. The front of his coat was spotted with a distasteful combination of cigarette ashes and dandruff.

Swiping absently at his lap, he blew out a long stream of blue smoke and looked around.

After watching him closely for five minutes, Jerry was positive that this was the man he'd been waiting for. He stood behind his counter shifting his weight from one foot to the other like a racehorse eager to be let loose. Finally, when he could stand the tension no longer, he took a deep breath and braced himself as he prepared to round the corner of his display and venture out onto the floor.

Just then a woman with the girth of a revolving door, wearing a blue and white striped sack dress confronted him. "Oh, excuse me," she said. "Do you carry skeleton costumes—in his size?"

And she pointed to a boy, evidently her son, with the body of a rain barrel. His leisure suit was cut from the same cloth as his mother's trend-stopping dress.

"I'll be right back, madam," Jerry shrilled hysterically as he circumnavigated her bulk. "It's possible we do. Add up his waistline until I get back."

Leaving the woman to vent her wrath on the part-timer, Jerry meandered through the crowd and struggled his way over to Helene's counter. The man with the beret was walking along the rows of model airplanes and trains, passing by the brightly colored boxes without really paying attention.

Helene was repairing the stuffed animal display after weathering a particularly boisterous onslaught of Girl Scouts. She didn't notice Jerry when he first approached.

"Helene," he said as he pulled the #4 envelope from his pocket. "I need a favor—" He glanced over his shoulder for an instant and turned back to face her.

As soon as she recognized his voice, Helene dropped what she was doing and whirled to bore her most savage stare right through his heart. But he was such a disheveled mess that she figured she'd tear him apart later and bear with him just one last time.

"What's the matter?" she asked, and then stated in her usual tactful manner, "You look terrible."

Jerry fidgeted and stole a glance over his shoulder again. "I know. I haven't got time to—"

But Helene cut him off defensively. "I didn't mean that in the sense that I'm going to invest myself emotionally in any effort to make you look better." She threw down an armful of koala bears and armadillos.

"I wouldn't want that," Jerry tried to explain. Instinctively, he picked up a fat, feathery duck and held it to his chest. "But thanks."

"Y'know," Helene said, eyeing him suspiciously. "In the storeroom there's an entire orgy of animals you can relate to." She tore the fluffy duck from his fingers and tossed it into the bin at the other side of her display.

"Orgy? Come on, Helene," Jerry beseeched her. "This is important."

But what was important to Jerry was not necessarily important to Helene. "Do you know where I was last night?" she asked in a suggestive, almost accusatory voice.

"Oh, God!" Jerry wailed and tore wildly at his own hair.

"In a singles bar," Helene continued, right through his anguish. "All by myself."

Jerry leaned against the counter and stood up on his toes to find the man with the beret. After spotting him next to the bubble-making machine, he turned back to Helene.

"I'm talking life or death," he almost screeched in frustration, "and you're talking loneliness. Helene, listen to me—please."

Helene held her right hand out in front of her and waved an incriminating finger in his face. This mild commotion caused her imposing breasts to tremble beneath her tight turtleneck sweater. The resulting shimmy did not go unnoticed by the appreciative male clerks nearby.

"Hold on a second." she shouted at Jerry. "Do you think I came out of that bar all by myself?" Then she answered her own question before Jerry could even inhale. "Wrong! I went home with maybe the most beautiful man I've ever met. I mean inwardly, of course."

At last her mind caught up with her mouth and she stopped talking. She closed one eye and narrowed the other as she searched Jerry's harried face for some explanation.

"What do you mean, 'life or death?' " she asked.

"I can't explain it," Jerry said, relieved at finally having gotten through to her. "Just do one thing for me." He pointed toward the bubble-making machine. "Look over there."

Helene followed his gesture and waited. "Uh-huh."

"The man wearing the beret—" Jerry said carefully. "Just give him this note and walk away."

"That's it?" she asked as she took the envelope from him.

"That's it, Helene," Jerry said. "Thanks."

Not quite undertsanding what all the fuss was about, Helene shrugged her shoulders and made her way across the *Bambini* floor. Heads turned and admired her provocative shape as she weaved her way toward the bubble-making machine.

As soon as she started across the floor, Jerry crouched behind her counter and crawled to the other end. Then, partially hidden by the stuffed giraffe, he peeked around the side and watched as Helene walked up to the man with the beret.

When she reached him, his back was to her and she had to lean in close to tap him on the shoulder. The man turned around slowly, a quizzical expression on his face. Then he smiled pleasantly when he saw the voluptuous Helene standing there. His eyes drifted uncontrollably to her irresistable endowments and he smiled even more broadly.

Helene simply handed him the envelope, turned on her heel, and walked away.

As soon as Jerry witnessed Helene passing the message, he hurried through the crowd and passed through the swinging doors of the corridor leading to the pay phone. The fish had bitten the bait and it was time to call Jenny.

The man in the beret watched Helene's bottom as she went back to her counter. Then he looked at the envelope in his hands. He turned it over and over in his palm.

"*Qu'est-ce que c'est?*" he muttered to himself as he took off his beret and scratched his head.

"Perhaps I can be of some assistance," Herbert Little said as he took the envelope from the hand of the unsuspecting Frenchman.

XXVII

The features of the Frenchman's face warmed from puzzled dismay to pleasant surprise when he turned toward his benefactor. "*Excusz-moi, monsieur.*" he said diffidently. "I don't speak the English—uh, *parlez-vous Français?*"

Herbert Little, dressed splendidly in a three-piece beige gabardine suit and an elegant brown topcoat, held out his hand and said humbly, "*Comme ci, comme ça.*" He wiggled his gloved hand to indicate his command of the French was only moderately passable. A fresh white carnation pinned to his lapel provided just the right exclamation point to his sartorial confidence.

The man in the beret smiled at the American's humility and pointed to the envelope Herbert had just taken from him. "*Qu'est-ce que c'est que ceci?*"

Inserting the slender tip of one gloved finger beneath the flap, Herbert opened the envelope and removed a sheet of paper. After reading its message, he glanced up and announced with a show of disdain for the material in his hand, "*Ah, oui, monsieur. C'est un—*" he pretended to search for the proper word. "*C'est un—*advertisement," he stated in a schooled French accent.

But the Frenchman was still perplexed.

"For the store," Herbert explained as he flashed the envelope briefly before the other man's eyes. "*Uh, per le magasin.* To buy toys. *Uh, Acheter les jouets.* Advertisement. *Uh, publicité."*

The man in the beret leaned back and laughed heartily as if sharing a joke with a new friend. *"Ah, publicité. Merci, monsieur."*

Herbert laughed along with his new friend and made a grand show of tearing the advertisement in half. The Frenchman put his finger to his temple and twirled it in tiny circles as if to agree that it was indeed a crazy idea. Then, still chuckling to himself, he clapped his friend Herbert on the back and walked away.

As soon as the Frenchman disappeared into the milling crowd, Herbert slipped both pieces of the note into his coat pocket and headed directly for the coffee shop.

At about the same time, Jerry was growing more flustered over the fact that nobody was home at his apartment. He let the phone ring ten more times and then, disgusted and consumed with worry, slammed the receiver back on the wall.

He stood in the corridor thinking through the problem and finally decided to go home to investigate. It wasn't like Jenny not to have at least called him if she were going to go out. Something must be wrong, he concluded.

Jerry darted down the hallway and pushed his way through the teeming mass of shoppers as he struggled to get to the escalators. Just as he was about to step onto the down escalator, he spotted Jenny coming up the other one. His heart soared with relief.

Jenny waved to him and smiled as the moving staircase carried her up to the third floor. She was wearing a tight, white blouse tucked into new blue jeans and a short, navy blue, hooded jacket.

It took all the resolve Jerry could muster to keep from gobbling her up with a tremendous hug when she came to the top of the escalator. Instead, he took her hand and squeezed it tightly.

"I couldn't help it, Jerry," she said as she took his

hand in both of hers. Her eyes implored him to understand. "I called here but they said you were too busy to come to the phone. I just couldn't sit there." She lowered her voice as she pressed against him. "I wanted to be with you."

Forcing himself to retreat a few steps so as not to appear too intimate while on the job, Jerry said, "I almost went out of my mind!" Then he stopped. Something was wrong. Something was missing. He looked around, trying to figure out what was unusual. Then it struck him.

"Where's Benjamin?" he asked.

"I took him to Flora's apartment in the Bronx," Jenny responded calmly. "That's what took so long."

"Flora?" Jerry said in dismay. "What did she say?"

Jenny let out a small laugh. "She was actually grateful." She said she was going crazy only dusting her own things." But she discerned that Jerry was still worried. Although she wanted to put him at ease, part of her was gratified that he cared so much for her son. "He'll be fine there, Jerry."

"But didn't she ask how come you weren't in France?" Jerry wanted to know as he pulled her aside to allow a rush of customers access to the escalators.

"I told her Preston had to leave without us," Jenny replied. "She of course gave me one of those ten-ton, packed-with-meaning looks."

"I know, I know—'men.' " Jerry mimicked an old lady, raising his eyebrows and frowning severely.

While Jenny laughed at this, grateful for a much-needed lighter moment, Jerry suddenly tensed. The man with the beret had just emerged from the crowd around Helene's counter and was headed for the escalators.

"That man wearing the beret," Jerry whispered urgently as he pointed. "Do you know him?"

Serious now, Jenny followed his finger and eyed the Frenchman carefully. After a moment, she shrugged her shoulders and simply said, "No."

"Well, he's either the killer or a messenger," Jerry said, the excitement rising in his voice. He watched as the man in the beret stepped onto the down escalator.

"He just picked up the instructions," he explained as the Frenchman passed from sight. "So far the plan's working. The store closes in about twenty minutes." He released her hand. "Just wander around like you're shopping."

Jerry winked at her and turned to weave his way through the last-minute customers as he headed for his department. When he worked his way through the last of the crowd, his heart sank. The fat lady in the blue and white strips and her color-coordinated chubby son were still standing there waiting for the skeleton costume.

The woman seemed unperturbed and the boy was patient enough. But Jerry Green was contemplating suicide.

XXVIII

After waiting for the last patron to leave the public men's room next to the coffee shop, Herbert Little slipped into the last booth against the wall and latched the door. Then he removed the two halves of the torn message from his coat pocket and held them next to each other as he flattened them on the wall. His eyes narrowed and he clenched his teeth in anger as he read the long letter. Written crudely in thick red pencil, the message began:

I WILL ACCEPT $25,000 IN CASH
FOR THE JEWELS, NO QUESTIONS ASKED.
OBEY THE FOLLOWING INSTRUCTIONS
EXACTLY AND . . .

Most of the customers had made their purchases and had cleared out of *Bambini* by that time. A series of bells chimed throughout Macy's to signal the imminent closing of the store for the evening. Jerry was absently rearranging the mess on his counter top, relieved to finally have a little breathing room after the unusually heavy shopping day.

Jenny watched a couple of kids wage a fierce tank battle on a video game set and then wandered over toward Jerry's department. "What do we do when the store closes?" she asked softly while pretending to be

191

interested in the holster and pistol set Jerry was trying to stuff back in its box.

"We stay out of sight somewhere until nine-twenty," he said out of the side of his mouth without looking up. "I guess the best place to hide is at the movies. If there's something decent playing." Jenny didn't laugh. She was too wrought up with a jangling case of nerves. "Then at nine-thirty, I have to be waiting in a phone booth."

Out of the corner of his eye he caught a glimpse of his supervisor crossing the floor with Helene. Although the supervisor's attention was understandably riveted elsewhere, Jerry automatically switched on his faithful Macy's-employee routine.

"This is our most popular model," he bragged loudly as he removed the pistol from its holster and showed it to Jenny. "It's genuine cast iron and completely harmless—unless it falls on your foot."

But the supervisor was interested in other, bigger things and he passed by without even glancing at Jerry. After he'd gallantly held the lounge door open for Helene and passed from sight, Jerry slipped the cap pistol into the outside pocket of his sport coat.

From his vantage point behind the menu blackboard in the coffee shop entrance, Herbert Little observed Jenny Moore talking intimately with Jerry on the other side of the floor. It was all beginning to make sense to him now. The connection was clear. He stepped back into the dining area to plot his next move. Preston Moore's wife and the Macy's salesclerk were involved and he'd have to do something about it.

Unaware that he was being spied upon, Jerry continued to outline his plan to Jenny. "The notes are already planted around the city," he said, his confidence growing now that it seemed his scheme was finally getting under way. "The instructions we passed to the man in the beret give him the phone number of the booth near the park."

Although Jenny was more worried than ever, Jerry's eyes sparkled with the promise of adventure. "He calls me at exactly nine-forty and I tell him where to find the first note," he went on as he outlined the rest of the plan. "That one tells him to leave the $25,000 there and then to get to the next note. And so on." He stood back proudly, his chest puffed out just a trifle, and waited for the heaps of praise he knew would be coming from the woman he loved.

This was the first time Jenny had heard of any money being involved and her mind locked onto it. It seemed to mean only more trouble to her. "What 25,000?" she asked. "Jerry, what are you talking about?"

"That's so he'll believe this is for real," he explained, still assured of the inviolable brilliance of his method.

But Jenny was not quite as convinced as he was. "It's crazy!" she wailed, her eyes darting back and forth nervously. "Suppose he hasn't got $25,000? Suppose he doesn't follow the notes at all?"

Jerry let out a long, exasperated breath. It was essential to him for Jenny to have unequivocal faith in his scheme. "I have a contingency plan for that unlikely eventuality," he said quickly, before she could ask any more difficult questions. "Okay, if he doesn't leave the $25,000, I'll still have plenty of time to remove the final note—the one that tells him where the jewelry is. It's all in his instructions."

This back-up plan was far from satisfactory for Jenny. "You mean you're a shadowy figure lurking after a killer in Central Park while all this is going on?" she demanded. Her worry was beginning to evaporate under a severe attack of panic. "Jerry, we're going to the police." She reached for his hand.

"Wait! This is brilliant!" Jerry protested as he grabbed her outstretched hand and held her captive until he finished speaking.

"The plan then is for me to telephone the police as soon as I'm sure he's picking up the notes," he explained. "The final note sends him right back here. Harvey Chortles is downstairs, sitting on a swing in the store window." He squeezed her hand urgently, hoping she'd respond. He waited. She stayed quiet.

"So, when he gets here to break the window," he continued more slowly now as if listening to it all the way through for the first time himself. "The police'll be ready and waiting and—" The spark abandoned his eyes. "—and it's the worst plan that ever got put together in all recorded history," he moaned as he dropped her hand.

Just as Jenny was about to come around the counter to urge him to leave with her, he raised his head and told her, "Okay, don't worry about a thing because I have a foolproof, fail-safe, contingency plan."

Jenny eyed him skeptically, disappointment etching its way across her face.

He looked into her disillusioned eyes and said softly, "We're going to the police."

Her eyes brightening, Jenny gave him a quick hug and once again felt better about her man, his plan, and his instincts.

Jerry reached into his coat and removed his cassette recorder. "We'll tape the entire story first and leave it with my lawyer for protection. And then we'll go to the police. Only one thing wrong with that."

"What?"

"I don't have a lawyer," he admitted as he suffered another setback to yet another ill-conceived but inspired plan.

"I do," Jenny said.

Rescued once again, Jerry was momentarily charged with energy. "Then, that's it! And we'll—" But the thunder left him as quickly as it had come. "They'll never believe us in ten million years," he groaned.

"We can try," Jenny urged. "There's nothing else left for us to do. Jerry?"

He had placed both hands on his counter, his head

bent over desposdently. It had all caught up with him and he was ready to concede. He turned to face her, the pain of failure weighing him down.

Jenny put her hand on his and folded her fingers into his. "You know the wisest move I ever made?"

"No."

"Dropping those pretzels all over the floor here the other day." Jenny pressed close to his side and kissed his ear. "I love you."

His spirits partially buoyed by Jenny's faith, Jerry took her hand and led her across the floor toward the back stairwell. There was only a handful of customers completing their transactions and the store had grown uncommonly quiet in the past few minutes.

They paused at the fire door. "But where should we go?" Jerry asked.

"I don't know. Somewhere to make the tape recording," Jenny suggested. "How about my lawyer's office? I'll call him." She reached for the door.

"No, wait," Jerry said as he pulled her back. "Let's stay right here in the store. We can make the tape and—" he looked earnestly into her eyes, "—and we can have one whole night together. All right?"

"But how can we stay here?"

Jerry knew she was going to ask that. It was only logical. "I'll show you. Come on." And he guided her back across the floor toward the outdoor playthings display.

Herbert Little watched every move they made from behind the coffee shop counter.

In the middle of all the swing sets and jungle jim mazes stood a fully assembled sheet metal playhouse. The size of a small room, it was constructed to look like a fairy tale cottage with white shingles, a red chimney and false bay windows.

Jerry led Jenny past the sporting goods department and stopped at the low door of the playhouse. After glancing around to make sure that the few sales clerks who still remained were all occupied at their counters, Jerry whispered, "Okay, now."

Jenny stooped down and ducked into the playhouse. Once again checking that none of the employees was paying any attention, Jerry swiftly followed her inside.

It was dark in the playhouse and the metal walls and floors augmented the sounds of their movements into a hollow echo. They crawled to the farthest corner of the structure and gathered together as much of the wooden baby furniture as they could reach so that they were able to construct a frail, but comforting barrier against the outside world. Then, slightly nervous but cozy in their corner, they held each other tightly and waited for the store to close.

As soon as the few straggling salespeople finished with their evening procedures and began to trickle toward the elevators, Herbert Little came out of the coffee shop. Moving stealthily, his senses keen and alert, he crept over to the sporting goods department. After watching the last clerk leave the floor, he dove under a pool table and joined in the waiting game.

XXIX

Snuggled around each other in the corner of the playhouse, Jerry and Jenny rested their heads against the back wall and listened to the muffled sounds from downstairs as Macy's was being closed for the night. Doors were locked, the escalators were stopped, and a resounding electronic click accompanied the sudden darkness as the powerful fluorescent lighting system was shut down.

Only a few conventional light bulbs burned dully throughout the building, casting a twilight aura on the third floor. Jenny cocked her ear and listened intently for any indications of movement in the store. Convinced that they were completely alone, she shifted around on her hip to speak to Jerry.

But he quickly put his fingers to her lips. "There's a night watchman," he whispered. "Wait till he makes his rounds."

Herbert Little smiled and silently thanked Jerry for his whispered warning.

The slender funnel of brightness from Cappy's flashlight cut the darkness and alerted everyone on the third floor to his approach. Jerry pulled his knees up to his chest and squeezed even closer to Jenny. It wasn't often that Cappy did a thorough job of inspecting the toy department, but Jerry wasn't taking any chances. The security captain had been coming down pretty hard on Cappy lately.

His body coiled and tense, Herbert Little slipped a long switchblade knife from his pocket and flicked it open. He lay close to the ground and watched as the old man moved past the playhouse and ambled slowly toward the pool table.

Jerry could feel Jenny breathe a small sigh of relief as Cappy's footsteps passed their hiding place. He turned his head to listen as the night watchman continued his rounds. Just when he was about to let Jenny know that everything was safe, they heard a strange, unidentifiable noise and then a muted thud. Confused, they looked to each other for an explanation. But their looks suddenly turned to fear as they heard the footsteps approaching the playhouse again. This time the stride was quick and purposeful.

A pair of legs appeared in the low doorway and Jenny let out a gasp. She fidgeted in her place and seemed ready to cry out when Jerry put his hand over her mouth and tried to calm her. Her eyes bulged in terror as she silently pleaded with him to remove his hand.

As the man in the doorway began to crouch, Jerry dropped his hand from her mouth and they both gasped involuntarily. Herbert Little appeared in the opening, a pistol with a long silencer held loosely in his hand.

"Hello, Mrs. Moore," he said with a sneer as he pointed the sinister-looking pistol into the playhouse. "I trust Mr. Moore has recovered from the flu by now," Herbert chuckled softly.

Having expected to be confronted with nothing more threatening than the harmless Cappy, Jerry was taken by surprise when this stranger showed himself in the doorway. As soon as he eyed the menacing weapon in this intruder's hand, his surprise changed to terror.

"Who the hell is that?" he asked Jenny in a high-pitched voice.

"Jenny's shoulders sagged as she said resignedly, "Preston's secretary." The key to the puzzle.

Herbert poked his gun inside so that the two of them would know he meant business. "I think you'd both better come out of there," he suggested patronizingly. When they didn't move, he cocked the gun with his thumb and shouted, "Now!"

It was all the prodding Jerry and Jenny required.

XXX

Jerry helped Jenny to her feet and allowed her to go first. As soon as she stepped in front of him and obscured Herbert's line of sight, he stuck his hand inside his coat and turned on his cassette recorder.

"Excuse me," Jerry said, after Jenny had passed through the doorway. "Is that item you're pointing at us an actual real gun with a silencer on the end of it that you could use to kill both of us and nobody would even hear it?"

A wry smile spread across Herbert's face. He appreciated a man with a sense of humor. "That's exactly what it is."

Jerry rose to a crouch and pushed the baby furniture side noisily. "That's an exceptionally persuasive item you've got there. Make room for me too."

He joined Jenny by the front of the playhouse and shook the cramps out of his legs. The few security lights throughout the store cast an eerie palor on the various shapes and angles that comprised *Bambini* at night.

"Well!" Jerry exclaimed heartily as if trying to make everyone feel comfortable at a party. "So you're Preston's secretary!"

Herbert couldn't help but like him. A man cracking jokes at gunpoint; it was something he himself might have done if he were unfortunate enough to find himself on the wrong end of the barrel.

"That's right," he said, an amused glint in his eye. Then he waved the pistol to the right. "Let's walk over there," he suggested.

Jenny stared at him coolly. She'd finally discovered her husband's killer, and the notion of Preston's having been murdered by someone who professed to being such a close and respected friend vexed her. She stiffened and refused to move.

Intuitively, Jerry understood Jenny's seething wrath. But he also understood that provoking Herbert would probably be the biggest and last mistake of their lives.

Before Jenny could say anything, he grabbed her hand and started toward the sporting goods section. Herbert fell into step behind them.

"So, how are things at the office?" Jerry asked as gaily and as lightly concerned as two friends bumping into each other at lunch.

Herbert didn't care to talk shop. "Turn right," he commanded.

They obliged and came into full view of the pool table. Cappy lay spread beneath the table's legs, the switchblade knife plunged up to the hilt in his back. His legs were splayed awkwardly and his hat had fallen near his feet.

Jenny recoiled at the dreadful sight and let out a tiny scream. She covered her face with both hands and stood trembling in the soft light. Jerry put his arms around her and tried to comfort her as he guided her toward the camping equipment counter. When he got to the display of flashlights, cookware, dart boards, darts, cooking gas and other outdoor paraphernalia, he turned around to face Herbert. Jenny turned with him and shuddered with disgust when she saw Cappy's hat in the aisle.

"Just stand there. That's fine," Herbert said, the pistol still trained in their direction.

Jerry put his hand into his pants pocket, and in so doing, caused his sport coat to fall farther open. It all seemed quite innocent to Herbert, but Jerry knew exactly what he was doing. The microphone for the tape recorder was now better exposed for more accurate recording.

"That's the night watchman, there, isn't it" Jerry asked.

Herbert was unmoved by Jenny's vitriolic stares or Jerry's continued prying. In fact, he seemed almost bored with the task ahead of him.

"Yes, it is," he answered, without bothering to look back at Cappy.

Jerry nodded and went on. "And he's dead, right?"

"That's right."

"So that's probably your knife sticking out of his back, isn't it?" Jerry was pressing his luck and he knew it. But if Herbert Little and his pistol were not kept distracted, they just might get down to other, more dangerous pursuits.

"Right again," Herbert winked.

"Which, of course, means that you killed him," Jerry postulated. It was becoming more difficult, but he forced himself to keep an unconcerned, almost happy, lilt in his voice.

"Yes, I did," Herbert stated and strode over to Cappy's body. Keeping the gun aimed at Jerry and Jenny, he knelt beside the night watchman and tugged his knife out of the old man's back. Then he wiped the blade clean on Cappy's uniform jacket and closed the knife. He dropped the switchblade into his coat pocket and rose to return to his captives.

"What's his name?" Jerry asked Jenny while Herbert was still at the pool table.

She bristled like an alley cat and spit out his name through clenched teeth. "Herbert Little."

When the killer arrived before them, Jerry took one calculated step forward and said loudly, "Okay, what do you want, Mr. Little? We haven't got all night!"

To Jerry's and Jenny's relief, Herbert continued to find Jerry's reckless bravado amusing.

"Agreed," he smiled. "I'd like you to hand over the jewelry to me." He raised his gun and Jerry shrank back against the counter. "It's that simple."

"Exactly what jewelry are you talking about?" Jerry asked. He could feel Jenny inch sideways toward him and he put his arm around her waist protectively.

"If you mean *my* jewelry," he held out his arm. "I'm tarnished up to the elbow from my wristwatch alone." He shook his head as if to advise Herbert against making a bad deal. "You don't need it," he counseled.

For one of the few times in his life, Jerry's relentless stream of one-liners was paying off. Herbert Little actually laughed at his joke.

"Look at that! He's laughing!" Jerry exclaimed to Jenny in mocking and wild-eyed appreciation. Then he came around to face Herbert again.

"You just killed somebody and you're standing there laughing!" he said, the first traces of his displeasure creeping into his voice. "You're a maniac, you know that? But go ahead, anyway. What jewelry did you have in mind?" His last question was thrown at Herbert like a challenge.

"All right, we'll get this as clear as possible," Herbert said. His mood was darkening in direct proportion to Jerry's and his patience was waning. "The Frelinghuysen jewelry."

Jerry made a feeble attempt at letting out an uninterested chuckle. "Yeah? Well, why didn't you say so in the first place? What makes you think we have the Frelinghuysen jewelry?" He chortled nonchalantly as if Herbert were wasting his precious time. "We don't have it. No way in the—"

Herbert let Jerry ramble on as he took the torn envelope from his pocket. He held it up for all to see.

"Oh, that," Jerry said hollowly.

"You were going to try to lead me on a childish treasure hunt right into the arms of the police." Herbert returned the message to his pocket and snorted contemptuously. "What an incredibly simple-minded idea."

It hadn't seemed so at the time, but in the light of recent events, Jerry had to concede that Herbert did have a point. "That I'll have to grant you," he admitted.

"So now I'd appreciate it if you'd just hand over the jewelry," Herbert said.

Jerry had one last card to play. "Suppose we don't?" he dared.

Calmly, with unequivocal meaning, Herbert raised the pistol until it was pointing directly at Jerry's forehead.

"I'll kill you," he said without emotion.

"You mean—you mean if I give you an absolute, one-hundred-percent, unqualified no—" His voice was wavering now. "You'll—kill us?"

"Just try me," Herbert said evenly.

"Right here?" Jerry demanded with as much idignation as he could muster. "In the toy department?"

"Look, my friend," Herbert Little began irritably. Jerry had pushed him to the brink. "I've already killed four people for that jewelry—"

"Five," Jerry corrected. Jenny braced herself for the worst as he itemized Mr. Little's escapades and counted each one on his hand. "Mrs. Moore's husband, Ernest and Audrey Van Santen, Frank Danziger. And now the night watchman over there. All with knives in the back." He held out his hand, the five fingers spread apart, each representing one of Herbert's victims. "That's five. Correct me if I'm wrong. I'm rotten in arithmetic."

"No, you're right," Herbert conceded. "That's five." He seemed almost pleased with his accomplishments.

"So two more won't make any difference, will they?" Jerry said offhandedly. Jenny shivered at the thought and dug her nails into his hand.

"None at all," Herbert replied ruthlessly.

"Uh-huh." Jerry took a long thoughtful pause, as if to ponder the alternatives. "Then I guess we'd better give it to you," he said at last.

"That would be wise, young man," Herbert agreed. He relaxed his trigger finger slightly.

"It's right here in the store, so it's really no problem," Jerry said casually. He noticed Herbert ease up on the trigger. "I mean we'll just all go and get it and give it to you."

"A splendid idea," Herbert allowed. "Let's just do that."

"Consider it done," Jerry said cooperatively. "But I have a couple of questions first. Sheer curiosity is all it is, mind you."

They'd all been standing in one spot for quite some time and Jerry began to fidget as he spoke. "You were Mr. Big of this all-dead group of jewel thieves," he surmised. "So my question is, how come a bigshot like you was Preston Moore's secretary?" He held up his hand to keep Herbert from responding. He had the floor and he intended to play it for all it was worth.

"And I think I can answer that myself," he said confidently. "He didn't even know you or Danziger at all. He only dealt with the Van Santens, who got him into this in the first place. Right?"

"Right." Herbert was impressed with Jerry's insightful reasoning.

"You know, you're an extremely intelligent man."

But flattery would do Herbert no good, Jerry went on with his indictment. "And so, once you weaseled your way in as his secretary, you didn't need him anymore. All the files on who owns what jewelry were available to you. Also, he was demanding a bigger cut."

It was almost as if Jerry were lecturing a classroom full of students about a particular problem in logic. He reconstructed each component, taking time to make his implications lucid, and then neatly wrapped it all up with a perceptive conclusion.

"So you stabbed him," he said, with the finality of a professor having just proved a difficult point through deductive reasoning. "The rest of the killings were out of sheer greed—and pretty disgusting if you don't mind my saying so. Am I right?"

Jerry's brilliance was only of passing interest to Herbert by then. "Unbelievable! You're right on the nose," he mocked. His mind was on one thing only. The jewelry. "If you're finished—and I suggest that you are— can we go get our little treasure now?"

Jerry knew that he'd exhausted his repertoire. "Yeah, let's do that." He gestured around the store. "We'll need some flashlights, though."

He turned around and grabbed the handle of a huge flashlight from the outdoor display counter. As he came around to face Herbert again, his body shielded his other hand. Jenny watched apprehensively out of the corner of her eye as Jerry's right hand closed around a cluster of heavy championship darts.

"This is your Sonny Jim Big Beam Special," he announced as he crossed toward his adversary. Herbert lowered his weapon just a trifle.

"It'll shine right through a brick wall," Jerry said as he came up close to the killer.

Suddenly, he flicked the switch with his thumb and the powerful beam of the heavy-duty flashlight blasted directly into Herbert's eyes. Stunned and blinded, Herbert raised the gun and tightened his finger around the trigger.

At that same instant, Jerry flung his handful of darts at Herbert. Most of them missed their mark, but one imbedded itself firmly in the wrist of his gun hand and a few others struck him in the arm and shoulders. Herbert screamed and writhed with pain. His shot went awry, blowing away the head of the stuffed giraffe as his gun clattered to the floor.

Moving instinctively, Jerry pulled the cap pistol from his pocket and levelled it and the flashlight at the hapless Herbert Little.

"Don't bend over for that gun!" he shrilled in a high, excited voice. "Or I'll shoot you through whatever part of your body you name!" Jerry poked the cap pistol at him. "Put your hands up!" he commanded. It was his turn to be in control.

After pulling the dart from his wrist, Herbert raised one hand over his head and lifted the other one to shield his eyes from the blinding light. Jerry motioned for Jenny to join him and then shouted at Herbert, "Now start walking backwards! Keep your hands where I can see them!"

Squinting and shading his eyes with his injured hand, Herbert said, "You haven't got a gun there."

"No?" Jerry said, cutting him off vigorously. "What do you call this, Mr. Smartass?"

Strutting forward, he shifted the beam of light from Herbert's eyes and trained it on the gun in his hand. Then he defiantly thrust the weapon in Herbert's face and held the cool metal up to his cheek.

But even Jerry's luck had its limits. Precisely at that moment, the pistol broke open, its barrel falling forward on a hinge, and its insides revealing nothing more deadly than an empty cap spool.

The toy gun wasn't even loaded.

XXXI

Time stood still.

It was a classic moment. A vicious killer with five notches on his gunbelt stood inches away from a toy department clerk who held a broken cap pistol in his hand. The gorgeous wife of the first murder victim stood behind her man, her face frozen in shocked disbelief. The muted hues of the security lights threw a macabre glow over the confrontation.

In that one tiny fraction of a second that must transpire before people can assimilate all the information thrust upon them and take action, the three of them responded in three very distinct manners. Herbert Little could think of nothing other than diving to the floor for his gun and coming up shooting. Jenny Moore's only consideration was escape. And the first thing that occurred to Jerry Green was another joke.

Having had far more experience at this sort of dangerous living, Herbert was the first to react. But Jerry was not far behind. As the killer made his move for his gun, Jerry automatically swung out with the heavy Big Beam flashlight and caught Herbert just above the left ear with a solid blow. As Herbert crumpled under the stunning impact, Jerry jumped on him and began pummelling him wildly with his fists.

But, despite all appearances, Herbert was a wiry scrapper and he gradually began to gain the upper hand as he fought back skillfully. One well-aimed punch struck Jerry on the forehead and sent him sprawling on his back. Temporarily free of his adversary, Herbert rose to his knees and looked around for his pistol.

He spotted it about two feet behind him and turned to grab it. When he spun around again, the gun in his hand, Jenny was standing above him. Before he could adjust, she let out a loud guttural scream and kicked him in the chest with her boot. The kick knocked the air out of Herbert's lungs and he fell back heavily, his eyes glazed and his chest sucking for oxygen. Jenny jumped over him and kicked the gun from his hand, sending it sliding away into the darkest shadows of the floor.

Then, still energized by the threat of danger, she knelt over Jerry and slapped him across the face. Hard. He was just beginning to come around, but Herbert was also stirring just a few feet away. Desperately, she tugged at Jerry's arms and brought him to a sitting position. Then she slapped him again and this time he came to his senses.

In another second, Jerry realized where he was and bolted to his feet. His first instinct was to do battle with Herbert, but the killer was already struggling to his knees. Without another moment's hesitation, Jerry grabbed Jenny by the wrist and together they ran off through the toy department.

Herbert's breathing painfully returned to normal and he groped around the floor for his gun. It was nowhere to be found. Bringing himself to a standing position, he reached into his coat pocket and pulled out his switchblade. He flicked it open, the blade glinting diabolically in the soft light, and moved off in the same direction as Jerry and Jenny. His eyes burned with rage.

Blazing the trail for them like an expert, Jerry hurtled through the swinging metal doors of the storeroom. They paused for a second to catch their breath and allow their eyes time to get used to the darkness.

"Where are we going?" Jenny asked, her chest heaving.

"I know this place like the back of my hand," Jerry said with authority.

He took her wrist and started to run. But he only went a couple of feet before they plowed into a stack of cartons and tumbled over a low conveyor belt. Scrambling to their feet, they kicked the boxes out of their way and dashed for the freight elevator.

Jerry slapped at the elevator button repeatedly with his open palm. "Guard! Guard!" he shouted at the top of his lungs, his voice echoing hollowly through the dark storage room.

"The guard's dead, Jerry! We saw him!" Jenny said as she too began whacking at the elevator button.

"No! There's another one. Down on the first floor—in a room—at a tv console!" he gasped. "Little tv monitors—all over the place—" He kicked the elevator door.

Jenny tugged at Jerry's jacket. "Jerry, if he finds that gun—"

"Guard!" Jerry yelled, his face against the elevator door, hoping his voice would travel down the shaft. "And suppose he doesn't find the gun?"

"He has a knife."

Jerry spun around and looked at her. "Right," he said quietly. Then his panic returned to its fever pitch. "Guard!" he bellowed. "There's another genuine, living, armed guard in this place. Guard! Probably taking a nap in the basement thinking Cappy has everything under control. Guard!"

Grabbing his arm and yanking him forcefully, Jenny pleaded, "Please! Please, let's just get out of here!"

Giving up on the unresponsive elevator, Jerry came up with a reckless alternative to flight.

"No! We've got to catch him!" he said.

This was the last thing in the world Jenny wanted to

hear. "Why?" she asked with dismay. "We know who he is. The police will—"

The swinging doors to the storeroom were thrown open with an ominous thud. Jenny stopped in mid-sentence and searched Jerry's eyes for help.

"That's why!" he said in a loud whisper. "Come on!"

Staying low, they retraced their steps back to the cartons by the conveyor belt. Crouching down, they stopped to listen They could hear Herbert stalking toward the elevator. Jerry ventured a peek above the boxes and saw Herbert's shadow across the room. The long blade of his knife shone dully in his hand. He moved carefully, deliberately, the knife held before him like a probe.

Ducking down again, Jerry whispered into Jenny's ear, "When I say 'now,' you scream like there's no tomorrow! Okay?"

She nodded solemnly.

After rehearsing the sequence of events in his mind, Jerry started to rise. But he paused. Timing was crucial and they couldn't afford any mistakes. He ran it through once more, took a deep breath, and stood up slowly.

Herbert was just arriving at the elevator.

In one swift, coordinated movement, Jerry flicked the switch that activated the conveyor belt. It hummed to life and began its bumpy glide toward the freight chute in the near wall. At the same instant, Jerry said, "Now!" and Jenny gave forth with a long, piercing shriek that reverberated through the storeroom. While her scream still echoed, Jerry heaved a huge carton toward the elevator and yanked Jenny up onto the conveyor belt. As Herbert whirled around in confusion, the box struck him in the shins and sent him sprawling to the floor.

Jerry jumped onto the belt and held Jenny tight. The

211

conveyor carried them rapidly to the chute and they ducked their heads as they passed through the narrow opening. This time Jenny shrieked without any prompting from Jerry as the two of them hurtled through the darkness at a terrifying speed. But her wailing was almost drowned out by Jerry's own screaming. Abruptly, they crashed into a pile of empty cartons on the first floor.

Flailing about madly to get their footing, they slipped and tumbled about until they came free of the boxes. They jumped up together, and after looking around for a second, Jerry yelled, "This way!" and the two of them raced off through the shadows.

Up on the third floor, Herbert regained his feet in an instant and hurried toward the sound of the conveyor belt. The echoes of Jerry's screams left little doubt in his mind as to which way his quarry had fled. After closing his knife and slipping it into his pocket, he dived headfirst through the opening and caromed down the chute. Herbert Little didn't scream.

Flinging the door open, Jerry and Jenny rushed into the security room. Television monitors lined one entire wall, offering clandestine views of various parts of the store.

"Guard!" Jerry shouted. "He's supposed to be here!" He ran to the washroom. "Guard! Police! Fuzz! Somebody! Anybody!" He came back to Jenny. "Sure, go find a cop in New York when you need one."

Then he noticed that she was holding a piece of paper in her hand. The fearful expression on her face told him that it wasn't good news. Without a word, she handed him the handwritten note she'd found on the desk.

Cappy, it read. *My stomach's a mess. Gone home. Call if you need me. Lock up. Walter.*

Before Jerry could even express his disappointment, Jenny poked him in the ribs and pointed at the monitors. "Look!" she said breathlessly.

On one of the television screens, they could see Herbert Little shoot out of the chute and smash into the cartons. He scurried to his feet and was reaching into his pocket for his knife when Jerry turned to run from the room.

"Come on!" he yelled, and dashed through the door.

Jenny watched the monitor as Herbert flicked open his knife. Then she spun around and hurried after Jerry.

Lost in the unfamiliar surroundings, Herbert turned around in a full circle trying to determine which way to continue his pursuit. Then he heard a motor sputter and rumble to life. Setting his jaw, he lowered his head and darted through the tall doors into the receiving dock area.

Loading ramps and high platforms angled off in every direction. A box shredder and enormous trashbins hulked beneath the gargantuan, corrugated iron garage doors. They could well have provided an excellent hiding place and Herbert, his knife at the ready, crept toward them.

Just then, a forklift came barreling out of the shadows as Jerry floored the accelerator and aimed the machine straight for Herbert. Jenny clung to the rollbar, her hair flying, as the vehicle bore down on their prey.

Herbert just had enough time to react and avoid a head-on collision. He jumped to the side and Jerry swerved the forklift at him, barely managing to sideswipe the elusive killer. The garage doors trembled loudly as Herbert was flung hard against them. But he wasn't injured, only stunned.

After the collision, Jerry lost control of the forklift and it screeched sideways across the slick concrete floor. Jenny lost her footing and Jerry just barely grabbed her before the loader slammed into several bales of shredded cardboard. Thrown clear by the impact, Jerry and Jenny scrambled to their feet and raced through the doors.

With Jerry in the lead, they tore down the stairway and through the basement door. The bowels of Macy's were a maze of enormous generators, compressors, furnaces, and air conditioning ducts. The ponderous machinery, spread out below the catwalk where they stood, seemed to go on for acres.

Jerry unlatched the thick chain that was hung across the top of the iron ship's ladder and started to climb down to the cellar floor. Jenny hesitated, not wanting to travel away from the relative safety of the street. Then she heard the loud crash of footsteps hurrying down the stairs behind her. Almost stepping on Jerry's hands in her haste, she stepped on the ladder and climbed and slipped her way to the floor far below.

Herbert broke through the door and spotted Jerry and Jenny scurring through the tremendous machines. He eyed a fire extinguisher clipped to the wall behind him and tore it from its hinge. Then he lifted the large metal cylinder over his head and hurled it toward the fleeing couple.

"Duck!" Jenny yelled and they threw themselves to the floor.

The fire extinguisher struck a furnace, bounced across the aisle and slammed into a steam compressor before clanging to a stop just inches from Jenny's foot.

"You call yourself a secretary!" Jerry shouted up to the catwalk. "You should be in the office transcribing dictation, you—you maniac!"

He helped Jenny to her feet and led her into the noisy air conditioner room.

Grabbing both sides of the ship's ladder loosely in his hands and propping his feet against the rails, Herbert Little lithely slid down the twenty feet to the cellar floor and landed in a crouch. Then he turned and gave chase toward the doorway he had seen them pass through. He ran surely, steadily, at last convinced of their whereabouts.

But just as Herbert Little was about to enter their last refuge, Jerry leaped up and threw the switch on the huge generator. The machine shuddered and groaned to a halt, and the entire basement was plunged into inky blackness as the lights blinked off. Scuttling on their hands and knees, Jerry dragged Jenny through the darkness as they crept past the stilled machines.

When they reached the ladder, they heard Herbert stumbling aimlessly about the cellar until he tripped over the fire extinguisher and cursed them viciously from the floor below.

As soon as Jerry and Jenny reached the catwalk, they tore through the firedoor and ran like crazy for the only part of the store where Jerry could feel at home.

This was jungle warfare now—life and death—and Jerry wanted to fight the last battle in his own jungle.

XXXII

Even in the dark, Jerry knew his way around *Bambini*. In the few moments they had before Herbert could find them, he quickly outlined his plan to Jenny. When each of them was reasonable certain of the scheme, they took their positions just as they heard the footsteps on the third-floor landing.

As Herbert cautiously pried the door open, he poked his head through the narrow opening to get his bearings on the gloomy floor. With a mighty heave, Jerry sent a thirty-foot-tall, stuffed green dragon toppling over onto its side. Helene's counter crumpled beneath its awesome weight as it crushed everything in its path. The very top of the dragon's neck smashed into the door and slammed it closed against Herbert's head. Jerry had measured it perfectly.

Wailing pitifully, Herbert shoved his shoulder against the door again and again until he was able to budge the reluctant dragon enough to allow him to free his throbbing head. One more shove and he was able to come into the toy department, only to be attacked by a gigantic Raggedy Ann doll that Jenny pushed down on him from the top shelf of a nearby display. She scooted away as Herbert fell beneath the bulk of the doll.

Bellowing epithets at the top of his lungs, Herbert disengaged himself from the tangle of arms and legs and dragon's tails, and skulked down the center aisle. He held the knife poised above him, ready to strike at the first thing that moved.

At the other end of the aisle, Jenny joined Jerry behind a ten-foot-high wooden rabbit. Like the Trojan Horse, it was mounted on a wheeled platform and, although it had a benignly innocent face, it weighed more than five hundred pounds. It had been on display for over fifteen years and none of the store's employees had the slightest notion what it was there for.

But Jerry and Jenny had found a purpose for the behemoth bunny. Leaning their shoulders against its backside and pushing together, they coaxed the massive toy into a squeaking roll. Slowly it gained momentum, and soon it was rattling and sliding down the aisle, heading directly for Herbert Little.

Poor Herbert barely had time to gasp when he saw this huge hare blasting at him from out of the shadows. The rolling rabbit caught him full in the midsection, sent him flying back over the dragon, and pinned him against the door with a terrible thud.

"Give up, Herbert!" Jerry yelled from his hiding place. "Even the rabbits are turning on you!"

But Herbert was being driven by the prospect of over a million dollars worth of jewels and he wasn't about to give up. Rubbing his sore shoulder, he kicked the bunny away and stormed down the aisle with fire in his eyes. When he came to an opening, he saw the shapely leg of a woman protruding from a display of costumes. He swooped upon it and viciously plunged his knife into the leg with all his power. But it was the hard wooden leg of a store mannequin, and to his surprise, the knife bounced off and cut deeply into his own hand. Howling with pain, he took the knife in his left hand and thrust his bloody right hand into his coat pocket. He swayed as he walked, stalking animalistically, wounded, and hungry for the kill.

A thundering noise preceded the cluster of bowling balls that came roaring down the aisle toward him. He was barely able to skip over the first few, but one smashed into his right foot. Then another bounced into his shin and several more struck his ankles and legs in rapid succession.

Dauntlessly pursuing, Herbert stormed at full speed down the aisle, rounded a corner and screamed into the sporting goods section. He never saw the volley ball net that was suspended across the floor. The net caught him full in the face and, even us his feet continued to churn, it twanged him back down the aisle into a bin of basket-balls that tipped over onto his chest.

Trying not to laugh at Herbert's misfortune, Jerry led Jenny down another aisle and crouched beside her to whisper the rest of his hit-and-run battle plan. Suddenly a shadow loomed over them and Herbert Little leaped off an air-hockey table and landed at their feet. He was battered, bloody, and bruised, but the hostility that burned in his eyes told them that he was far from beaten. With the razor-sharp switchblade held before him, Herbert slowly advanced, savoring his imminent victory as he closed in steadily, step by step.

Jerry and Jenny retreated with each step Herbert took, until, finally, they found themselves backed up against a wall of crates. The end of the line.

Jenny huddled close to Jerry and together they stared in numbed silence as he came closer and closer.

"Give up, Herb," Jerry said as soon as he found his voice. "You haven't got a chance." Herbert spit at them and kept coming. "You're not mad that I called you 'Herb,' are you?"

Seeing that Herbert Little was in no mood for conversation, Jerry reached up behind him and pulled down the first crate he could lay his hands on. Shakily elevating the box high above his head, he pitched it toward the advancing killer. But it fell short.

Bursting open on impact, the crate spewed forth tens of thousands of marbles of all sizes. Herbert never had a chance. His foot came down on a few hundred marbles and he skittered and slipped until his feet were rolled out from under him. He landed heavily on the small of his back and scrambled through the mounds of marbles for his knife.

Seizing upon the opportunity, Jenny grabbed an oversized butterfly net from the camping display and brought it down over Herbert's head and shoulders. The killer struggled helplessly against the confines of the resilient mesh.

Slipping his way across the marbles, Jerry took up a baseball bat and struggling to remain upright, he raised his arms high over his head. Then he closed his eyes, gritted his teeth, and whammed the business end of the bat onto the dome of Herbert's head. The killer let out a small whimper and slumped to the floor. He grunted a few times and then lapsed into deep unconsciousness.

The momentum of Jerry's mighty swing sent him skidding across the marbles. He clutched onto Jenny for support and the two of them went tumbling onto the floor.

They sat there for a moment, stunned and exhausted by the incredible ordeal they'd just survived. Still gripping the bat tightly in his left hand, Jerry reached over and picked up Herbert's knife.

"I can't believe it!" he gasped. "In my entire career as a full-time kid, that's the first clean hit I ever got." He closed the knife against his leg and dropped it into his pocket. "It was all the time 'bunt, Jerry, bunt'!"

Using the bat for leverage, he worked his way up to a standing position and bent over to help Jenny.

"Even when there was nobody on base," he panted, "it was always 'bunt, Jerry, bunt—you know you can't hit!'" He looked at Herbert's still form. "Home run!" he said proudly.

Jenny put both her arms around his waist and hugged him close. But something was in the way. Jerry reached inside his jacket and pulled out the cassette recorder.

"Jesus Christ," he said, still breathing heavily. "I hope I had the volume on high enough."

Taking the tape player from him and putting it in her own pocket, Jenny raised herself on her toes and kissed her man full on the mouth. This shut him up.

Jerry responded by gallantly stepping closer and reaching to gather her up in his arms. Instead, he slipped on the marbles and landed squarely on his rump.

XXXIII

The man selling hot chestnuts from his pushcart on the corner didn't even bother to look twice when Jerry and Jenny walked past pulling a shiny new red wagon. Evidently the sight of an unconscious man, bound with dozens of bicycle chains and a maze of combination locks, slumped in a wagon being pulled by a young couple, was not all that interesting to him. Either he'd seen it before, or he didn't want to get involved this time around.

Jenny held Harvey Chortles under her arm and took the tape recorder from her pocket. She pressed the play back button as the two of them strolled down Fifth Avenue, the dreaded Herbert Little bumping along behind them. There was a moment of static and then Jerry's voice came through clearly over the speaker.

". . . One-hundred-percent, unqualified no, you'll kill us?"

"Just try me," came Herbert's confident reply.

"Right here?"

"Look, my friend," Herbert's voice interrupted menacingly on the tape, "I've already killed four people for that jewelry—"

"Five," Jerry corrected.

They'd heard enough. Jenny clicked off the machine and slipped it back into her pocket. They reached another cross-street and rounded the corner. Now people were beginning to take some notice. Even for Manhattan, it was a bit peculiar to see a well-dressed man moaning beneath a mountain of bicycle chains in a Red Flyer Deluxe wagon.

Jerry switched the wagon handle from one hand to the other and draped his arm over Jenny's shoulder. She snuggled close and put her arm around her waist. Then she laid her head on his shoulder and squeezed him lovingly.

A group of cabbies was gathered at a taxi stand drinking coffee from steaming Thermos mugs. They turned to watch as the tiny caravan bounced its way toward the police station at the end of the block. Shrugging to each other as if such things happened every day, they sipped their coffee and went back to their sports pages and crossword puzzles.

The wagon groaned in protest as it tilted on two wheels when Jerry turned it down the path toward the Precinct Headquarters. Herbert Little's body shifted under the chains, but remained securely fastened in the bed of the wagon.

Inside the building, the desk sergeant looked up, thought he saw something outside, then returned to his ledger.

"Y'know, it just occurred to me," Jerry said to Jenny as they reached the glass doors of the police station. "On account of recording that maniac, I erased all my notes on the caterpillar book! Old Herbert's going to make me mad yet!"

"Don't worry, darling," Jenny smiled as she held the door open for him. "I left the combinations to all of these locks back at your store."

When he heard their laughter, the desk sergeant looked up and squinted at Jerry and Jenny, the teddy bear, the wagon, and their prisoner. Then, without batting an eye, he looked at the clock over their heads and remembered that it was time for his coffee break.

He pressed the intercom button on his desk and

called for the relief officer. Then he pushed his chair away and waddled down the hallway without ever looking back over his shoulder.

Left alone in the lobby of a Manhattan police stateion, Jerry and Jenny fell back on one of the wooden benches and waited.

They were together, they were safe, and they had nothing but time.